*"Told you so," Ric*

"Told me what?"

"That you could dance."

To emphasize the point, he gathered her close and spun her around the dance floor in a series of intricate steps that she followed without a single stumble. The color rose in her cheeks and the sparks returned to her eyes. By the time the music stopped, she was laughing.

"Okay, okay, I can dance, but only if I hang on to you for dear life."

"And the problem with that is?" he asked, his gaze locked with hers.

Her bright-eyed expression faltered. "You won't always be here," she whispered so low that he could barely hear her over the music.

Ricky wanted to deny it, wanted to tell her that she would always be able to turn to him, but the commitment terrified him. The only thing that terrified him more was the prospect of losing her.

Dear Reader,

While every romance holds the promise of sweeping readers away with a rugged alpha male or a charismatic cowboy, this month we want to take a closer look at the women who fall in love with our favorite heroes.

"Heroines need to be strong," says Sherryl Woods, author of more than fifty novels. "Readers look for a woman who can stand up to the hero—and stand up to life." Sherryl's book *A Love Beyond Words* features a special heroine who lost her hearing but became stronger because of it. "A heroine needs to triumph over fear or adversity."

Kate Stockwell faces the fear of knowing she cannot bear her own child in Allison Leigh's *Her Unforgettable Fiancé*, the next installment in the STOCKWELLS OF TEXAS miniseries. And an accident forces Josie Scott, Susan Mallery's LONE STAR CANYON heroine in *Wife in Disguise*, to take stock of her life and find a second chance....

In Peggy Webb's *Standing Bear's Surrender*, Sarah Sloan must choose between loyalty and true love! In *Separate Bedrooms...?* by Carole Halston, Cara LaCroix is faced with fulfilling her grandmother's final wish—marriage! And Kirsten Laurence needs the help of the man who broke her heart years ago in Laurie Campbell's *Home at Last*.

"A heroine is a real role model," Sherryl says. And in Special Edition, we aim for every heroine to be a woman we can all admire. Here's to strong women and many more emotionally satisfying reads from Silhouette Special Edition!

Karen Taylor Richman
Senior Editor

Please address questions and book requests to:
Silhouette Reader Service
U.S.: 3010 Walden Ave., P.O. Box 1325, Buffalo, NY 14269
Canadian: P.O. Box 609, Fort Erie, Ont. L2A 5X3

# Sherryl Woods

## A LOVE BEYOND WORDS

Silhouette

# SPECIAL EDITION™

Published by Silhouette Books

America's Publisher of Contemporary Romance

To Pat and Mark and all the others who went through
the travails of Hurricane Andrew right along
with me…here's to clear skies from now on.

**SILHOUETTE BOOKS**

ISBN 0-373-24382-0

A LOVE BEYOND WORDS

Copyright © 2001 by Sherryl Woods

This edition published by arrangement with Harlequin Books S.A.

® and TM are trademarks of Harlequin Books S.A., used under license.
Trademarks indicated with ® are registered in the United States Patent
and Trademark Office, the Canadian Trade Marks Office and in other
countries.

Visit Silhouette at www.eHarlequin.com

**Printed in U.S.A.**

# SHERRYL WOODS

has written more than seventy-five romances and mysteries in the past twenty years. And because she loves to talk to real people once in a while, she also operates her own bookstore, Potomac Sunrise, in Colonial Beach, VA, where readers from around the country stop by to discuss her favorite topic—books. If you can't visit Sherryl at her store, then be sure to drop her a note at P.O. Box 490326, Key Biscayne, FL 33149.

Dear Reader,

Readers often ask if I model my heroines after myself or other people I know. Most of my heroines are purely the product of my imagination, though once in a while something I see in the media strikes a chord and serves as the starting point for a character. Allie Matthews, the heroine of *A Love Beyond Words,* epitomizes the strong woman who has triumphed over fear and adversity. Allie lost her hearing, but instead of letting this trauma defeat her, she became even stronger. In *A Love Beyond Words,* I wanted to create a heroine who has taken hold of her life and is now strong enough to allow the hero into her life, to share the ups and downs with her and to share *his* ups and downs.

Another heroine I'm proud of is Anna Louise Perkins in *The Parson's Waiting,* a woman minister who had to defy incredible odds to work in an arena where women aren't so easily accepted. Anna Louise is reappearing as a character in my upcoming MIRA title *About That Man,* on sale in June 2001, where she is supportive of the heroine, who faces her own challenges as a strong woman.

My hope in creating heroines like Allie and Anna Louise is that they will become role models for you, the reader, as you face your own challenges in life. If you are having a similar problem or conflict in your life, I hope you will be encouraged by my heroines to say, "Hmm…maybe I can do that, too." Like you, my heroines are a complex combination of strengths and vulnerabilities, and like them, you can emerge triumphant from difficult situations.

I hope you will enjoy journeying with Allie Matthews to her happy ending, and that any issues you are currently struggling with will have a happy outcome, as well.

With all good wishes,

*Sheryl Woods*

## Chapter One

*Help me. Please help me.* The words echoed in Allison's head, though she had no idea if she had actually spoken them aloud.

Everything around her was eerily silent, but it had been that way long before Hurricane Gwen, with its 130-mile-an-hour winds, had struck Miami just after midnight. In fact, her world had been silent for nearly fifteen years now, a long time to go without hearing her parents' voices, a long time for someone who had studied music to miss the lyrics of a favorite love song…an even longer time to adjust to a life of perpetual quiet.

Watching the newscasts about the approaching storm, she had read the lips of the veteran meteorologist and sensed, rather than heard, his increasing panic over the size and force of the storm and its direct aim at Miami.

Then the power had gone out, and she had been left in total darkness to wonder what was happening outside. She'd tried to tell herself it was beyond her control, that she ought to go to bed and attempt to sleep, but for some reason she had stayed right where she was, on the living room sofa, waiting for morning to arrive. Unable to listen to a radio for updates on the storm's progress, she had simply replayed the last reports over and over in her mind and prayed she had done everything she could to protect herself and her home.

Anyone who'd lived in South Florida for any length of time knew the precautions to take. From the start of the hurricane season in the spring until it ended in November, they were repeated with each tropical storm that formed in the Atlantic.

Allie had arrived from the Midwest only a few months earlier, but she was a cautious woman. After living her whole life with the surprise factor of devastating tornadoes, she was grateful for the advance notice most hurricanes gave from the instant they began to brew off the coast of Africa. Unlike some newcomers, she took the potential threat of these powerful storms seriously.

At the very start of her first hurricane season, she had read every article on preparedness. She had installed electric storm shutters on her pretty little Spanish-style house before she'd spent a dime on the decorating and landscaping she wanted to do. She had a garage filled with bottled water, a drawer jammed with batteries for her flashlight, plus stashes of candles and canned goods. She had double what anyone recommended, enough to share with neighbors who weren't as prepared.

She suppressed a hysterical laugh as she wondered where all of those precious supplies were now, buried right here in the rubble with her, but defiantly out of reach and useless. As for the house in which she had taken such pride, there appeared to be little left of it but the debris that held her captive. Obviously, despite all she'd done, it hadn't been enough.

It was pitch-dark, though she couldn't tell for certain if that was because of the time of day or the amount of debris trapping her. She suspected the former since every once in a while rain penetrated the boards and broken furniture that were pinning her down in painful misery.

Every part of her body ached. She had cuts and scrapes everywhere. The most intense pain was in her left leg, which was twisted at an odd angle under the weight of a heavy beam. She had no idea how long she had been unconscious, but sensed it couldn't have been more than minutes. Her stomach still churned from the sudden shock of shutters ripping loose, windows blowing in and walls collapsing around her.

There had been no time to run. Perhaps if she had heard the wind and lashing rain, things would have turned out differently. Instead, out of the blue she had experienced the odd sense that the walls were quite literally closing in, and then everything had begun to break apart around her. Her house had seemingly disintegrated in slow motion, but even at that, she hadn't been able to move quickly enough.

She had taken one frantic step toward the safety of a doorway, then felt a wild rush of air as the roof lifted up, then shattered down in heavy, dangerous chunks. Those expensive shutters—which had wiped out the last of her savings—had been no protection at all against the fury of the storm.

She remembered the slam of something into the back of her head. Then her world had gone blissfully dark for however long it had been. When she'd come to, there had been nothing but pain. A foolhardy attempt to move had sent shafts of blinding agony shooting up her leg. She had passed out again.

This time she knew better. She stayed perfectly still, sucking in huge gulps of air and fighting panic. She hadn't been this terrified since the day nearly fifteen years earlier when she awoke in the hospital and realized that everything seemed oddly still and silent. Sensing that something was amiss, she had flipped on the TV, then tried to adjust the volume. At first she had blamed the television, assuming it was broken, but then she had inadvertently knocked over a vase of flowers. It had crashed to the floor without a sound. And then she had known.

Panicked, she had shouted for her parents, who had come running. They had brought the doctors, who had ordered a barrage of tests before concluding that nerves had been damaged by the particularly virulent attack of mumps she'd contracted.

For a while they had hoped that the effect would be reversible, but as time passed and nothing changed, the doctors had conceded it was likely that her world would forevermore be totally silent. It had taken days before the devastating news finally sank in, weeks more before she'd accepted it and slowly learned to compensate to some degree for the loss by relying on her other senses.

Now, because she couldn't see what was happening, it was as if she had suddenly lost yet another of her senses—her sight. She wasn't sure she could bear it if the inky darkness that was her world right now was permanent.

Frantic, Allie again shouted for help, or thought she did. In that great vacuum of silence in which she lived, she had no idea if anyone could hear her and was responding. She didn't even know if anyone was searching the area for casualties or whether the worst of the storm had passed or was still raging overheard.

She had no idea if the dampness on her cheeks was rain, blood or tears. On the chance that it was the latter, she scolded herself.

"Stay calm," she ordered. "Hysteria won't accomplish a thing."

Though, she conceded, it might feel good to give in to a good bout of tears and rage about now.

That wasn't her style, though. She hadn't valued or even tested her own strength before she'd lost her hearing. At nineteen she had cared more that she was pretty and popular, that her college studies in music education came easily. Then, in an instant, none of that had mattered anymore. She had been faced with living her life in total silence and she had been terrified. What would she do if she couldn't share her love of music with others? Who would she be if she couldn't perform in the occasional concert with the local symphony as she had since her violin teacher had won an audition for her when she was only fourteen?

For a time Allie had quit college and withdrawn into herself. Once gregarious, she had sought isolation, telling herself it was better to be truly alone than to be in a room filled with people and feel utterly cut off from them. Her parents had hovered, distraught, taking the blame for something over which they'd had no control.

Then one day Allie had taken a good, hard look at her future and realized that she didn't want to live that way, that in fact she wasn't living at all. Her faith had taught her that God never closed one door without opening another. And so, she had gone in search of that door.

Not only had she learned sign language, she had studied how to teach it to others. She might have lost something precious when the raging infection had stolen her hearing, but she had gained more. Today she had a career that was full and rewarding, a chance to smooth the way for others facing what she had once faced. The hearing-impaired children she worked with were a challenge and an inspiration.

The strength it had taken to view tragedy as an opportunity would get her through this, too. She just had to ignore the pain, the nearly paralyzing blanket of darkness, and stay focused on survival.

"Think, Allison," she instructed herself, calmer now.

Unfortunately, thinking didn't seem to be getting the job done. Determined to make her way to safety, she tried to maneuver one of the smaller chunks of debris on top of her, only to realize that the action was causing everything to shift in an unpredictable, potentially deadly way.

This time when the tears came, there was no mistaking them. They came in tandem with the pain and fear.

"I am not going to die like this," she said, then repeated it. She thought it was probably just as well that she couldn't hear the quaver she could feel in her voice. "Just wait, Allie. Someone will come. Be patient."

Of course, patience was not a virtue with which she was very well acquainted. Once she had accepted her hearing loss, she had moved ahead with learning sign language and lip reading at an obsessive pace. She seized everything in life in the same way, aware of just how quickly things could change, of how a sudden twist of fate could alter a person's entire vision of the future.

Now, just as it had been when the doctors had been unable to battle the infection that had cost her her hearing, it appeared her fate was in someone else's hands. She could only pray that whoever it was would hurry up.

"Come on, Enrique," Tom Harris taunted. "Let's see those cards. I could use the down payment on a new car."

"In your dreams," Ricky retorted, spreading his full house on the bench between them.

The other firefighters had gathered around to watch the high-stakes, winner-take-all hand between two men who were intense rivals for everything from women to poker winnings in their spare time, but dedicated partners when it came to rescue operations. Ricky's grin spread as Tom's face fell.

"Come on, baby. Show 'em to me," he said, tapping the bench. "Put those cards right down here where everyone can see."

Tom spread three aces on the bench, then sighed heavily. Just as Ricky was about to seize the cash, Tom clucked disapprovingly.

"Not so fast, my man. This little devil here must

have slipped my mind.'' He dropped another ace on top of the other three, then grabbed the pot. "Come to Daddy."

The other firefighters on the search and rescue team hooted at Ricky's crestfallen expression.

"Next time, *amigo*," Ricky said good-naturedly.

There would always be a next time with Tom. About the only thing Tom liked better than playing cards was chasing women. He considered himself an expert at both pursuits, though even he grudgingly admitted that Ricky was the one with a real knack for charming any female between the ages of eight and eighty.

"You may be lucky at cards, but I am lucky at love," Ricky boasted.

"It's those dark eyes and that hot Latino blood," Tom replied without rancor. "How can I compete with that?"

"You can't, so give it up," Ricky retorted, as always. "You can't match my dimples, either. My sisters assure me they're irresistible."

"Your sisters aren't exactly unbiased. Besides, they have spoiled their baby brother shamelessly," Tom retorted. "It's no wonder you've never married. Why should you when you have four women in your life who wait on you hand and foot? I'm amazed their husbands permit it."

"Their husbands knew I was part of the bargain when I allowed them to date my sisters," Ricky said. "And there are five women, not four. You're forgetting my mother."

"Saints forgive me, yes. Mama Wilder, who comes from the old school in Cuba where the husband is king and the son is prince. She's definitely had a part in shaping you into a scoundrel.''

Ricky grinned. "I dare you to tell her that."

Tom turned pale. "Not a chance. Last time I offended her precious son, she chased me with a meat cleaver."

"It was a butter knife," Ricky said with a shake of his head at the exaggeration. His mother might be a passionate defender of her offspring, but she wasn't crazy. Besides, she considered Tom to be a second son, which she felt gave her free rein to nag him as enthusiastically as she did Ricky or his sisters. She was still lecturing Tom about his divorce, though it had been final for three years now. If it had been up to her and her meddling, he would have been back with his wife long ago.

"Hey, guys, cut the foolishness," their lieutenant shouted, his expression somber as he hung up the phone. "We've got to roll. There's a report of houses down."

"Casualties?" Ricky asked, already moving toward his gear.

"No word, but it's the middle of the night. Some people might have gone to shelters, but outside the flood zones where evacuations were required, most stayed home to protect their belongings. Worst-case scenario? We could have dozens of families whose ceilings came crashing down on top of them as they slept. Clearly the construction in that part of town was no match for Mother Nature."

"Multiple houses?" Ricky asked. "I thought we'd lucked out. I thought this sucker had all but ended. Was it the hurricane or a tornado spawned by the storm?"

"No confirmation on that. Either way, it's trouble," the lieutenant said.

Within seconds the trucks were on the road, traveling far more slowly than Ricky would have liked. The main street in front of the station was ankle deep in water and littered with debris. Rain was still lashing from the sky in sheets, and the wind was bending nearby palms almost to the ground. Other trees had been uprooted, their broken limbs tossed around like giant pick-up sticks.

Street signs had been ripped from the corners, making the trip even trickier. With signs down and landmarks in tatters, it was going to take luck or God's guidance to get them where they needed to be, even though it was less than a mile from the station. He murmured a silent prayer to the saints that they would reach the devastated street before someone died in the rubble.

As if in answer to his prayer, the rain and wind began to die down. In a few hours the street flooding would begin to ease, but that was no help to them now. They crept along at a frustrating pace.

The scene that awaited them when they eventually reached the middle-class Miami neighborhood was like a war zone. Power lines were down, leaving dangerous live wires in the road. Here and there a home had miraculously escaped the worst of the hurricane's wrath, but those were the exception. Most of the two-storey houses had been leveled by the winds or by an accompanying tornado. Those that hadn't collapsed completely were severely damaged. Roof tiles had been stripped away, glass was shattered and doors had been ripped from their hinges. Another testament to lousy inspections and shoddy construction, Rick thought wearily as he surveyed the damage. Hadn't the city learned anything from Hurricane Andrew?

There was no time to worry about what couldn't be changed. With the precision of a long-established team, the firefighters assessed the situation, then split up. A call was placed to the electric company to get a crew on the scene. In the meantime, barricades were set up to prevent people from stumbling onto the area around the live wires.

A few people were walking around dazed and bloody, oblivious to the light shower that was now the only lingering evidence of Hurricane Gwen. Some of the paramedics set up a first aid station and began to treat the less severely injured, while others took their highly trained dogs and began to search for signs of life.

A woman who looked to be in her seventies, clutching a robe tightly around her, hobbled up to Ricky. She seemed to be completely unaware of the bloody gash in her forehead, though her expression was frantic.

"You have to find Allie," she said urgently.

"Your daughter, ma'am?"

"No, no, she's my neighbor." She gestured toward a severely damaged house. As Ricky and Tom headed in that direction, she trailed along behind. "She's a wonderful young woman and she's already been through so much. This house was her pride and joy. She just bought it a few months ago, and she's been spending every spare minute fixing it up, putting in flowers all around."

Her eyes shone with tears. "None of that matters,

of course. Houses can be rebuilt. Flowers can be re-
planted.''

"You say her name is Allie?" Ricky asked.

"Allison, actually. Allison Matthews."

As Tom went to get the equipment they'd need,
Ricky surveyed the collapsed structure in the early
dawn light. He opened his mouth to shout, but the
woman's frail hand on his arm stopped him.

"Calling out won't help," she said urgently. "She
won't be able to hear you. Allie's deaf."

As if the situation weren't complicated enough, he
thought, then reminded himself to treat it as he might
a rescue in a foreign country where he didn't know
the language. It wouldn't matter that he couldn't
communicate with this Allie in the usual way. He
just had to find her.

He circled the twisted pile of debris, looking for
any sign of the woman, any hint of where rooms
might have been. Would she have been in an upstairs
bedroom or downstairs?

Shadow, the highly trained dog at his side, moved
gingerly through the rubble, sniffing. Rick stood
where he was, waiting, letting Shadow do his part.
This was always the hardest part of a rescue, hanging
back, leaving it to the German shepherd to pinpoint
signs of life.

Finally Shadow stilled, whimpered, then barked.

"So, you found her, did you, boy? Good dog."

Shadow yipped excitedly, but didn't move, as if
he sensed that one tiny shift could be fatal.

"Let's get her out of there, boy," Ricky said. He
paused long enough to give a reassuring smile to the
neighbor. "Looks like we've located your friend.
We'll have her out of there in no time."

"Thank God," she said. "Allie's one of those special people put on this earth to show others the meaning of goodness. She's an angel, sure as anything."

Ricky didn't know a lot of women who could live up to such high praise. He tended to gravitate toward women who could best be described as free and easy with their affections, the kind who placed no demands on him, who knew that his job came first. Definitely not the sort of women to take home to meet his mother, who bemoaned his failure to marry on an almost daily basis. The only time she let up was when he brought Tom home for a meal of her famed pork roast, black beans and rice. Then she served up marital advice along with the food. Tom enjoyed her cooking too much to complain.

Of course, right now it didn't much matter whether Allie was a saint or a sinner. She was someone who needed his help, and that was all that mattered.

He intently studied the collapsed home again, looking for the best possible access, using Shadow's watchful stance as a guidepost to Allie's location.

"Shouldn't you hurry?" the elderly neighbor asked, wringing her hands anxiously.

"Better to do it right than rush and cause more injuries than whatever she's suffered so far." Thinking of his grandmother and how she would feel under these circumstances, he took a moment to cup the woman's icy hands. "It's going to be okay."

No sooner were the words spoken than he heard a feeble cry for help from deep within the rubble. The sound tore at his heart. Knowing that there was nothing he could say, that words of reassurance would quite literally fall on deaf ears, he settled for reassuring her friend instead.

"See, there? She's alive. We'll have her out of there in no time," he said optimistically. "In the meantime, why don't you go over to the first aid station that's been set up and let somebody take a look at that cut on your forehead. Looks as if you might have a sprained ankle, too."

"At my age, hobbling's normal. As for the cut, it's nothing," she said, facing him stubbornly. "I want to be right here when you bring Allie out. She must be terrified. She'll need to see a familiar face."

Ricky recognized the determined set of her jaw and gave up arguing. Like his *abuela,* this woman knew her own mind.

He looked around until he caught sight of Tom, who had assembled the necessary rescue equipment and was ready to get started.

"All set?" his partner asked.

Adrenaline kicked in as it always did when the hard work was about to begin. Ricky nodded.

"Let's do it," he said with an eagerness that always struck him as vaguely inappropriate. Yet it was that very anticipation that had driven him to take on such highly dangerous work in the first place. True, what he did sometimes saved lives, which was incredibly rewarding, but it also tested his skill and ingenuity at outwitting the forces of nature and near-certain death in the aftermath. A part of him craved that element of risk.

Often he was halfway across the world. Today, however, he was in his own backyard, so to speak. Somehow that raised the stakes.

He thought of the elderly woman's assessment of

Allie and grinned. He had to admit that his anticipation was heightened ever so slightly by the promise
than when this particular rescue was over, for the first
time he might be face-to-face with an angel.

## Chapter Two

Allie fell in and out of consciousness. Or maybe she only slept. She just knew that every once in a while her eyes seemed to drift shut and her pain faded away. When she awoke, there was always the throbbing, more intense than ever.

"Help!" she cried out again. Surely by now there were rescuers in the area. If they could hear her, they could find her. Gasping at the pain, she steadied herself, then shouted again, "Help!"

When her shouts were met with nothing but more of the same silence, she felt as if she were calling into some huge void. As her cries continued to go unanswered, she began to lose hope. What if they never found her? How long could she stay alive in this unrelenting heat without water? Despair began to overwhelm her.

Then, suddenly, just when she was about to give

up, she thought she caught sight of a faint movement
far above her. Was it possible? In the pitch-
blackness, she couldn't be sure. Had there been a
glimmer of light?

"Here," she called on the chance that it hadn't
been her imagination playing cruel tricks on her.
"I'm down here."

A chunk of what once had been her roof—or
maybe a wall, considering how topsy-turvy everything was—was eased away, allowing her a first
glimpse of sky. Ironically, given the storm that had
raged so recently, the sky was now a brilliant blue,
too beautiful by far for anyone to imagine that such
destruction had been wreaked by the heavens only
hours before.

Relieved that she still had her sight, she wanted to
simply stare and stare at the sunshine, but she was
forced to close her eyes against the brilliance of it.
Still, she could feel the blazing heat on her cheeks
and vowed she would never again complain about
Miami's steamy climate. It felt wonderful.

When she finally dared to open her eyes again,
there was a face peering back at her, the most handsome face she had ever set eyes on. Of course, at
this point, she would have been entranced by a man
with whiskers down to his knees and hair the con-
sistency of straw if he'd come to save her. This man
was a definite improvement on that image.

Even with his hard hat, she could see that he had
black hair, worn a little too long. He had dark, dark
eyes and a complexion that suggested Hispanic her-
itage and dimples that could make a woman weep.
It was all Allie could do not to swoon and murmur,
"Oh, my."

He was too far away for her to read his lips with any accuracy, but she could see his mouth slowly curve once again into that reassuring, devastating smile. She clung to the sight of that smile. It was a reminder that life could definitely be worth living. No man had smiled at her like that in a very long time, if ever.

Or maybe she just hadn't noticed, she admitted candidly. From the moment she'd lost her hearing, her life had taken on a single focus. Everything had been about learning to adjust, learning to cope, opening that new door...and forgetting about the social life that had once consumed her. She discovered that not many men were interested in a woman who couldn't hang on their every word, anyway.

For fifteen years now she had had male colleagues, even a few men she counted as friends, but not a single one of them had made her blood sizzle the way this one had just by showing up. She figured it had to be a reaction to the circumstances. After all, this hardly seemed to be an appropriate time for her hormones to wake up after more than a decade in exile.

As time slid by, she kept her gaze locked on that incredible face. She sensed from the way the debris was slowly shifting above her that there was a scramble to free her, but that one man stayed right where she could see him, easing closer, inch by treacherous inch.

"Hi, Allie," he said.

By now, he was close enough that she could read his lips. And she guessed from the way he'd spoken, being so careful to face her, that he knew she was deaf.

"Hi." She breathed the word with a catch in her voice, even as relief flooded through her. It was going to be okay. As long as he was there, she knew it.

"Can you read my lips?"

Eyes glued to his face, she nodded.

"Good." He reached out his hand. "Can you take my hand?"

She tried to move her arm, but it felt as if it, too, were weighted down, just like her pinned leg. She almost wept in frustration.

"That's okay," he said. "Hang in there a little longer. You're being incredibly brave, and if you give us just a little more time, I'll be able to reach you and this nightmare will be over."

She nodded.

"Anything hurt?"

"Everything," she said.

He grinned. "Yeah, dumb question, huh?"

He turned his head away. She could see a change of expression on his face and guessed he was speaking to someone out of sight.

More debris shifted and bits of plaster rained down on her. She yelped, drawing his immediate attention.

"Everything okay?" he asked, his expression filled with concern.

She nodded, her gaze locked with his worried brown eyes.

"Good. Then here's the deal, Allie. I imagine you want to know what we're up to out here, right?"

"Yes." She wanted to know everything, even if she didn't like it. She'd learned a long time ago that she could cope with just about anything as long as she knew what she was up against.

"Okay, then. I'm going to disappear for just a minute. We're not happy with this approach, so we're going to come in a different way. It'll take a little longer, but there's less risk. Are you all right with that?"

She wanted to protest the delay, but he was the one who knew what he was doing. She had to trust him. Gazing into his eyes, she found that she did. And even though she didn't want him to move, didn't want to lose sight of him, she nodded again. "Okay."

She turned her head away to hide the tears that threatened. Suddenly she felt what seemed to be a deliberate dusting of powder sprinkle down on her face. She glanced up to find him watching her anxiously.

"Sorry," he apologized. "I needed to get your attention. I promise you'll see me again in no time. I never leave a pretty woman in distress."

She almost laughed at that. Even when she wasn't under a ton of debris, no one in recent years ever said she was pretty. Now she imagined she must look a fright. She had been dressed for bed when disaster struck, wearing a faded Florida Marlins T-shirt and nothing else. At the end of the day, her hair was always a riot of mousy-brown curls, thanks to Miami's never-ending humidity. She imagined she looked pretty much like a dusty, bloody mop about now.

"Go," she told him. "I'll be here when you get back."

He chuckled. "That's my girl."

And then he was gone, leaving Allie to wonder if

it was possible that angels ever came with dancing eyes…and looking like sin.

Ricky was still chuckling as he eased his way off the mound of debris. Allie Matthews was something, all right. Scared to death but doing her level best not to show it. He'd caught the occasional glimpse of panic in her amazing blue eyes, but not once had she complained. She had to be in pain, as well, but beyond her one joking admission, she'd never mentioned it again.

"You find something funny about this?" Tom asked, regarding him with curiosity as he leaped to the ground beside him.

"You probably had to be there," Ricky admitted.

"How's she doing?"

"Her sense of humor's intact, but she can't move. No way to tell if that's because she's pinned down or because of an injury. Bravest woman I ever saw, though. She's not hysterical, but those eyes of her are killers, blue as the ocean and shimmering with tears, though she's fighting them like crazy."

Tom shook his head. "Leave it to you to go all poetic about a woman's eyes in the middle of a rescue."

"I was hoping to motivate you," Ricky claimed, though the thought of Tom getting ideas about Allie bothered him more than he cared to admit. It was crazy to be jealous over a woman to whom he hadn't even been introduced.

He gazed at the rubble with frustration. "Any idea how we can get in there without bringing this mess tumbling down around her?"

They stood surveying the crazy haystack of debris.

It was far from the worst they'd ever seen. There had been whole apartment complexes to dig through in earthquake disasters. But Ricky had never felt a greater sense of urgency. Something about Allie's spirit and bravery had caught his attention in a way that few women did. In just a few minutes he had felt some of that strength and resilience that her neighbor had bragged about.

For the next few hours Ricky, Tom and the others worked with tedious patience to reach Allie. When they finally had a clear view of her through a tunnel that seemed safe enough, Ricky was the one who inched forward on his belly, clearing more debris bit by bit until he could reach out and touch her hand. Again those huge, luminous blue eyes latched on to him and held him captive.

He passed a water bottle to her, but she couldn't seem to negotiate it to her mouth. She stared at her immobile hand with evident frustration.

"It's okay," he soothed. "I'll get it to you. Hang in there."

He eased forward an inch at a time, waiting between movements to make sure that the precarious arrangement of debris wouldn't shift. Finally he was close enough to touch the plastic straw to her lips. She drank greedily, her gaze never leaving his face.

"Is Jane okay?" she asked the minute she'd satisfied her thirst.

"Jane?"

"Next door. Mrs. Baker."

He thought of the woman who'd guided them to Allie. "About seventy-five? Five-two? Feisty?"

"Yes, yes, that's her. She's okay, isn't she?"

"A cut on her forehead and possibly a sprained

ankle, but you're the only thing that seems to concern her," he said. "She hasn't budged since we started trying to reach you. She found a lawn chair down the block and planted it right out front so she can keep an eye on us."

Allie grinned. "That sounds just like her. And the rest of the neighbors? How are they?"

"We're checking on all of them now," he said, unwilling to mention that so far there was one dead and several unaccounted for. Fortunately, she seemed to take his response at face value.

"How long have I been down here?" she asked.

"Not so long. A few hours. We got the call shortly before six a.m. It's just about noon now," he told her. "Must seem like an eternity to you, though."

She nodded.

"Well, it's almost over. You stay perfectly still, *querida*. I'll have you free in no time," he promised.

"Couldn't move if I wanted to," she said as a tear slipped down her cheek. "I—" her voice faltered "—I think I might be paralyzed."

"Now, don't go getting any crazy ideas. Looks to me as if it's just because of the way you're wedged in here," he reassured her. "No need to panic. Once you're out, I'll take you dancing."

The teasing drew a watery smile. "You'll regret it. Even before this I had two left feet. On top of that I can't exactly hear the music."

"I'll take you someplace where it only matters if you can swivel your hips."

"Ah, salsa," she said knowingly.

"With a little tango mixed in," he said. "You'll just have to hang on and follow my lead."

She gave a decisive little nod. "I can do that."

"Then it's a date."

All the while he talked, chattering nonsense mostly just to keep her attention focused on his face, he cleared debris from on and around her. When he saw the bloody gashes in a long shapely leg, he had to fight to keep his expression neutral.

That was the worst of it, though. If he could free her leg, he thought he could get her to safety. He just had to keep his mind on what he was doing and off the fact that she was all but naked. The T-shirt she'd presumably worn to bed was shredded indecently. She apparently hadn't noticed that yet or else she was more brazen than he'd imagined.

"Make sure there's a blanket ready and waiting when we come out," he murmured into the radio tucked in his pocket, his head turned so she couldn't read his lips. She tapped his shoulder, her expression frustrated. He smiled. "Sorry. I was talking to my partner. I just wanted to be sure he'd be ready for us when we blow this cozy little cave under here."

It took another hour of careful excavation around her leg before he felt confident enough to move her.

"You ready?"

"Oh, yes," she breathed softly.

"I'm not guaranteeing there won't be some pain."

"What else is new?" she said bravely.

"You want something for it?"

"Just get me out," she pleaded.

He cradled her as best he could, aware of every bare inch of skin he was touching, then slowly worked his way back the same way he'd come. It seemed to take forever, but at last he saw Tom's face peering at them intently.

"You have that blanket?"

"Right here."

Ricky reached for it, then wrapped it around Allie as best he could in the confined space, before shimmying the rest of the way out.

Allie blinked against the brilliant glare of sunlight and continued to cling to Ricky as if he were all that stood between her and an unfamiliar world.

And, of course, the neighborhood must seem strange—nothing like what it had been the last time she'd seen it before the storm. Ricky could only imagine how it must feel to emerge and find everything changed. He'd seen that same sense of shocked dismay on the faces of other victims of other tragedies as they realized the extent of the damage around them and the likelihood of casualties among their friends and family.

As for the way Allie was looking at him and holding on, it wasn't the first time he'd seen that reaction, either. The bond between victim and rescuer could be intense, but in most instances it wasn't long before familiar faces arrived and the bond was broken.

This time, though, only the elderly neighbor stepped forward to give Allie a fierce hug, even as the paramedics moved in to begin their work. Allie was on a stretcher and headed for an ambulance in no time, Jane right beside her, giving instructions. Ricky grinned at the bemused expressions of the paramedics at taking their orders from a pint-size senior citizen in a flowered housecoat and bright-pink sneakers.

"Wait," Allie commanded as they were about to lift her into the ambulance. Her gaze searched the crowd.

Ricky felt a quick rush of heat at the precise moment when she spotted him. Her gaze locked on his.

"Thank you," she mouthed, too far away for him to actually hear the words.

"You're welcome," he said, then deliberately turned away from the emotion shining in her eyes to move on to another complicated search taking place a few houses away.

"You going to see her again?" Tom asked as they began work on the recovery of a victim who had been less fortunate than Allie.

"I wasn't down there making a date," Ricky retorted.

"I was asking about your intentions."

Those blue, blue eyes came back to haunt him. He wondered if he might not have to see her again before he could get them out of his head.

"I promised to take her dancing," he admitted, earning a punch from Tom.

"Next time there's a pretty woman involved, I get first dibs," Tom said. "There's nothing like a little gratitude to get a relationship off to the right start."

"And what would you know about relationships, Mr. Love 'Em and Leave 'Em?"

"More than you," Tom said. "I was married."

"For about fifteen minutes."

"Three years," his friend corrected.

"And in that time you learned what?"

"That women get all crazy once you put a ring on their finger."

Ricky chuckled. "Are you referring to the fact that Nikki thought you ought to stop dating other women after the wedding?"

"Very funny. You know it wasn't that. I might

have looked, but I never went near another woman during that whole three years. Nikki just got all weird about the job. She knew what I did for a living when we met, but for some reason after we got married she seemed to think I'd give it up and go to work for her father.'' He shuddered. ''Me, behind a desk. Can you imagine it?''

No more than he could imagine himself there, Ricky conceded. ''Mama says Nikki still loves you.''

''Not enough to give up that crazy idea,'' Tom said, a hint of something that might have been sorrow in his eyes. But it was gone in a flash, replaced by an irrepressible glint of laughter. ''That divorce was the best thing that ever happened. Women figure if I got married once, I might risk it again. You'd be amazed what a woman will do when she's optimistic about your potential. You should consider it.''

''What? Get married, just so I can divorce? Not me. If and when I ever take the plunge, it's gonna have to be forever. Between Mama and the priest, my life wouldn't be worth two cents if I even breathed the word *divorce*.''

''Which is why you never date a woman for more than two Saturday nights running,'' Tom concluded. His expression turned thoughtful. ''I wonder if Allie Matthews could make you change your mind.''

''Why would you even say something like that? I barely know the woman, and you didn't exchange two words with her.''

''I got a good look at her, though,'' Tom said. ''A man doesn't soon forget a woman who looks that incredible even after being buried under a collapsed building. Besides, if her neighbor is right about what an angel she is, she's nothing at all like your usual dates. Did you ever consider that you make the choices you do precisely because you know they're not keepers?''

Ricky scowled at the analysis of his love life. He had a hunch it was more accurate than he wanted to believe. ''We've got more houses to check out,'' he said, stalking away without answering Tom's question. His friend's hoot of knowing laughter followed him.

What if he did protect himself from winding up married by dating women he would never, ever spend the rest of his life with? What was wrong with that? It wasn't as if he led any of them on. As Tom said, Ricky rarely went out with the same woman more than once or twice, and he always put his cards on the table, explaining that in his line of work he was on the go way too much to get seriously involved.

Maybe it was a pattern he'd developed to avoid commitment, but so what? It was his life. He liked living alone. He liked not being accountable to anyone. After spending his first eighteen years accountable to an overly protective mother, an iron-willed father and four sisters who thought his love life was their concern, he liked having his freedom. His nieces and nephews satisfied his desire for kids, at least for the moment. He got to play doting uncle, soccer coach and pal without any of the responsibility that went with being a dad.

There wasn't a woman on earth who could make him want to change the life he had.

Satisfied that Tom was totally and absolutely wrong, he dismissed his taunt about Allie Matthews. He'd probably never even see her again, never make good on that promise to take her dancing. She wouldn't even expect him to.

He was still telling himself that the next day, but he couldn't seem to shake the image of Allie's cerulean gaze as it had clung to his. If what he'd seen in her eyes had been expectations, he might have run the other way, but that hadn't been it. There had been gratitude, but underlying that there had been a vague hint of loneliness.

He tried to imagine being rescued from the debris of his home, having only an elderly neighbor for support, rather than the huge, extended family he had. He couldn't. He knew without a doubt that his hospital room would be crowded with people who cared whether he lived or died, people who would help him to rebuild his home and his life. Who would be there for Allie?

He spent an hour telling himself that surely a woman described as an angel would have dozens of friends who would be there for her, but he couldn't shake the feeling that Allie might not.

"Damn," he muttered, slamming his coffee cup into the sink and grabbing his car keys.

On the drive he told himself that if he got to the hospital and found that Allie had all the support she needed, he would just turn right around and leave. That would be that. End of story. End of being haunted by those big blue eyes.

Unfortunately, something in his gut told him he was about to go down for the count.

## Chapter Three

Allie hated the hospital. The antiseptic smell alone was enough to carry her straight back to another time and place when her life had been forever changed. This time she was an adult and her injuries weren't either life-threatening or permanent, but the doctors still had no intention of releasing her until she could tell them she had both a place to go and someone to care for her.

Unfortunately, there was no one. She knew only a few of her neighbors, and their lives and homes were in as much a shambles as her own. Her parents had offered to fly down immediately and stay with her, but the expense of paying for hotel accommodations for all three of them struck Allie as foolish. In addition she knew that they would hover just as they had years ago. She didn't need that. She needed to get back into a familiar routine as soon as she was physically able to. She had promised to let them know if she couldn't come up with another solution. There had to be one. It just hadn't occurred to her yet.

"What about that lovely young woman at the clinic?" Jane asked helpfully. She had been to visit the night before and was here again, taking a bus from her sister's, where she had been staying since the storm.

"Gina has a brand-new baby and a two-bedroom apartment. I couldn't possibly impose on her and her husband," Allie said, though her boss had indeed come by and issued the invitation.

"I would insist that you come to Ruth's with me, but she's not in the best health herself and, to be perfectly honest, she's a pain in the neck," Jane said.

Allie bit back a laugh. Jane's opinion of her sister was something she had heard with great regularity since she'd moved in next door to the elderly woman. They barely spoke, because Jane thought Ruth spent way too much time concentrating on her own problems and not nearly enough thinking of others.

"Old before her time," Jane often declared. "She was a cranky old woman by the time she hit fifty. Dressed like one, too. I tried to talk her into a snazzy pair of red sneakers the other day. You would have thought I was trying to get her to wear a dress with a slit up to her you-know-what."

Now she sighed. "The minute I get that insurance check, I'll move to an apartment, so I won't have to listen to her complaining all the livelong day."

"She did open her home to you," Allie reminded her. "She was right there as soon as she heard about what had happened."

"Yes, she was," Jane admitted. "Of course, she said it was her duty. She wouldn't have come, I promise you, if she hadn't worried what her pastor would think of her if she left her only sister on the street."

Jane waved off the topic. "Enough of that. We need to decide what's to be done about you. If I thought we could find an apartment in time, you could move in with me until you rebuild, but there's no way I can get settled someplace that fast."

"It's very sweet of you to want to do that, but this isn't your problem," Allie told her. "I'll figure something out."

Jane looked as if she wanted to argue, but eventually she stood. "Okay, then," she said with obvious reluctance, "but I'll be back tomorrow. Same time. You have my sister's phone number. If anything comes up and you need me, you call, you hear me? Any time, day or night."

Her elderly neighbor bent down and brushed a kiss across Allie's cheek. "I think of you as the granddaughter I never had, you know. I hope wherever we end up, we don't lose touch."

"Not a chance," Allie promised, squeezing her hand.

She watched as Jane left, admiring her still-brisk step in her favorite pink shoes. She wore them today with an orange skirt and flowered shirt. A bright-orange baseball cap sat atop her white hair. It was an outfit that could stop traffic, which Jane counted on, since she hated wasting time on a corner waiting for a light to change. It was a habit that scared Allie to death.

All in all, her neighbor was a wonder, interested

in everything and everyone. Allie saw her pause in the hallway and watched her face as she carried on an animated conversation with a nurse she'd befriended on her first visit. Jane had all of the doctors and nurses wrapped around her finger. Allie didn't doubt that Jane was the reason they'd been taking such extraspecial care of her, bringing her treats from the cafeteria and lingering to chat to make up for the fact that she'd had so few visitors.

Once Jane was gone, Allie struggled to her feet, determined to take a walk around the room at least to begin to get her strength back. She closed the door on her way past so no one would witness her awkward, unsteady gait.

She was still limping around the confined space, filled with frustration, when the door cracked open and eyes the color of melted chocolate peered at her. When her visitor spotted her on her feet by the window, a grin spread across his face.

"You're awake. They told me not to disturb you if you were sleeping."

"Come in," she said, glad to see her rescuer again so she could thank him properly for saving her life. "I just realized that I don't even know your name."

"Enrique Wilder," he said. "Ricky will do."

"Thank you, Enrique Wilder."

He looked almost embarrassed by her thanks. "Just doing my job."

"So you spend your life scrambling around like a cat saving people?"

"If I'm lucky," he said.

She shuddered a little at the implications of that. "Well, I'm grateful."

He moved carefully around the room, his gaze everywhere but on her. He seemed so uneasy, she couldn't help wondering why he had come. He paused to gaze out the window, and after a moment she tapped him on the shoulder so he would face her.

"Why are you here?" she asked finally.

"To tell you the truth, I'm not entirely sure."

"So this isn't follow-up you do on everyone you've pulled from a collapsed structure?" she teased lightly.

He looked away. She could see his lips moving, but because of the angle of his head, she couldn't read them. She touched his cheek, turning his head to face her.

"Oh, sorry," he apologized. "I forgot. I just came to make sure you're okay. No lasting damage?"

"None. You can check me off as one of your success stories."

"When are they springing you?"

"Not fast enough to suit me," she said.

"I thought the goal these days was to get people out as quickly as possible, too quickly sometimes."

"That's the general rule, yes, but these are unusual circumstances. It seems I don't have a home to go to, and they don't want me alone."

"You don't have a friend you could stay with?"

"None I feel I could impose on. I haven't been in Miami very long. Most of my friends are neighbors." She shrugged. They both knew the situation most of her neighbors were facing.

"Of course. How is Mrs. Baker, by the way?"

"Living with her sister and grumbling about it," Allie said with a chuckle. "Jane is very independent. She thinks her sister is a stick-in-the-mud. A half hour ago, you could have heard all about it."

His devastating smile tugged at his lips. "She was here?"

"Yesterday and today. She says it's to check on me, but I think she's just desperate to get away from her sister."

"I know the feeling," Ricky said.

"You have a sister?"

"Four of them."

Fascinated by the idea of such a large family, Allie sat on the side of the bed and regarded him eagerly. "Tell me about them."

He looked doubtful. "You can't really want to hear about my sisters."

"I do," she assured him. "I was an only child. I've always been envious of big families. Tell me about your parents, too. Is your mother Cuban?"

"How did you guess?"

"Your coloring and your first name are Hispanic, but your last name is Wilder. Those looks had to come from somebody."

He laughed. "Ah, deductive reasoning. Yes, my mother is Cuban. She met my father at school when she had just come to the United States. She swears she fell madly in love with him at first sight."

"And your father, what does he say?"

"He says she didn't look twice at him until they were twenty and he'd used up all his savings sending her roses."

Allie chuckled. "Maybe she just liked roses."

"That was part of it, I'm sure, but Mama has always understood the nuances of courtship. She might have been madly in love, but she wanted my father to prove his love before she agreed to a marriage that would be forever."

"And the roses proved that?"

"No, but the persistence did."

"And she passed all of this wisdom on to her children, I suppose, assuring that all of you have nice, secure relationships."

"Let's just say that my sisters each made their prospective husbands jump through hoops before they said yes. On occasion I felt sorry for the poor men. They had no idea what they were getting into. Sometimes I tried to warn them when they showed up for the first date, but it was too late. My sisters are very beautiful, and the men were already half in love with them before they arrived at the house."

"How about you? How have you made your mother's wisdom work for you?" she asked, surprised by how much she wanted to know if Ricky Wilder was married or single and how very much she wanted it to be the latter.

"I haven't. Haven't met a woman yet I wanted to impress."

"But I'm sure you're swimming in eager admirers," she said, teasing to hide her relief.

"What makes you think that?"

"Please," she chided. "Look in the mirror."

His grin spread. "Are you trying to say that you think I'm handsome, Allie Matthews?"

"Facts are facts," she said, as if she were stating no more than that. She hardly wanted him to know that he was capable of making her blood sizzle with little more than a glance. "Back to your sisters. Tell me about them."

He settled into the room's one chair. "Let's see, then. Maria is the oldest. She's thirty-six and has four children—all boys, all holy terrors. Each of them is fascinated by bugs and snakes and chameleons. To her horror, they're constantly bringing their finds home and letting them loose in the house. I told her it's penance for all the rotten things she ever did to me as a kid.''

Allie laughed, sympathizing with the other woman's dismay. ''How does she handle it?''

''She gives her husband and the boys exactly five minutes to find the missing creature and get rid of it.''

''And if they fail?''

''She leaves and goes shopping. She can buy herself a lot of perfume and lingerie in a very short period of time. She claims her skill with a credit card is excellent motivation for her husband.''

''I don't know,'' Allie said doubtfully. ''Some husbands might consider the prospect of a little sexy lingerie as a benefit, rather than a threat.''

Ricky grinned. ''I know. I don't think she's figured that out yet.'' His expression sobered. ''Then again, maybe she has. Maria is a very sneaky woman.''

''And the others?'' Allie prodded.

''Elena is next. She's thirty-five and is married to a doctor. They have only one child so far, because they waited until her husband's medical practice was well established before starting a family. My mother prayed for her every day. She will not be happy until there are enough grandchildren to start their own school.''

''Are the other two sisters cooperating?'' Allie asked eagerly, already able to envision the noisy family gatherings.

''Daniela and Margarita are twins. My mother despaired of ever getting them both married, because they took their own sweet time about it. Neither married until they turned thirty and had their own careers. Daniela is a stockbroker. Margarita is a teacher. Daniela has two daughters and insists that she's through. Margarita has a son and a daughter, but she's expecting again and the doctor thinks it might be twins. Needless to say, my mother is ecstatic.''

''I think I would love your mother,'' Allie said wistfully. ''And your sisters. I love my parents dearly, but they never anticipated having children at all. They're both college professors and loved the quiet world of academia. I came as a total shock to them. Not that they didn't adore me and give me everything a child could possibly want, but I always knew that I was a disruption in their lives. They would be horrified if they knew that I'd sensed that.''

Ricky's gaze narrowed. ''Do they know you're in the hospital?''

''Yes, and before you judge them, they did offer to fly down, but it's the beginning of the fall semester.''

''So what?''

''I couldn't ask them to do that. It would disrupt their classes.''

Ricky stared at her incredulously. ''You can't be serious. That's why they're not here?''

''They're not here because I told them not to come,'' Allie said defensively. ''We would have ended up in a hotel, anyway. It just didn't make sense.''

''You've just been through a terrible storm,'' he said indignantly. ''Your house was destroyed. You're in the hospital. They should have been on the next plane, no matter what you said.''

Allie refused to admit that a part of her had hoped they would do exactly that, but she had known better. They had taken her at her word, because it had suited them. It didn't mean they didn't love her. They were just practical, and they'd never been especially demonstrative except for those weeks after she'd lost her hearing. That it had taken such a thing to get their attention had grated terribly.

''I won't defend my parents to you,'' she said stiffly.

He seemed about to say something more but fell silent instead, his expression troubled.

Allie waited, and eventually he met her gaze.

''What will you do?'' he asked.

''Stay here a day or two longer, I imagine. Then the insurance company will no doubt insist the hospital kick me out no matter what. Or I suppose they could send me to an intermediate treatment center of some kind for rehab if the insurance would cover it.''

''A nursing home? At your age?''

''There aren't a lot of options,'' Allie said. ''Besides, I don't think it will come to that. I'm getting stronger every minute.''

''I saw you limping when I came in here. You're probably not even supposed to be on your feet, are you?''

The doctors had insisted on a few days of bed rest for her ankle and knee, but she didn't have the luxury of waiting. She had to prove she was capable of managing on her own. ''It's nothing,'' she insisted.

''I could ask your doctors about that,'' he challenged. ''Would they agree?''

She frowned at him. "Really, you don't need to worry about it. You did your job. I'll manage."

"Allie—"

"Really," she said, cutting off his protest. "It's not your concern. The social worker is looking into some possibilities."

"I can just imagine," he said dryly. He stood up, then moved to the window to stare outside as if something out there fascinated him.

Allie used the time to study him. Even if he hadn't been the one to rescue her and carry her out of the rubble, she would have recognized his strength. He was slender, but the muscles in his arms, legs and shoulders were unmistakable in the snug-fitting jeans and T-shirt he wore.

More important, there was strength of character in that handsome face.

As she watched, it was evident that he was mentally struggling with himself over something. She didn't doubt that it had to do with her. He seemed to be feeling some misplaced sense of responsibility for her predicament and nothing she'd said thus far seemed to have lessened it.

Finally he faced her and spoke very deliberately. "I have a solution."

"To what?"

"Your situation," he said with a touch of impatience.

"Which is?"

"You need a place to stay."

She told him the same thing she'd said to Jane earlier and to him repeatedly. "It's not your problem. I'll work it out."

"I'm sure you will, eventually, but you'd like to get out of here now, right?"

She couldn't deny it. "Of course."

"Okay, then. You could come home with me."

She wasn't sure which of them was more startled by the invitation. He looked as if he wanted to retract it the instant the words left his mouth. If she wouldn't impose on her friends, she surely wasn't about to impose on this man whose duty to her had ended when he saved her life.

"That's very kind of you, but—" she began, intending to reassure him.

"It's not like I'm there a lot," he said hurriedly, cutting off her automatic protest. "But I'd be there enough to satisfy the doctors, and it would be a roof over your head till you figure out what you want to do."

Before she could follow her first instinct and turn him down, he seemed to reach some sort of decision. His chin set stubbornly.

"I'm not taking no for an answer," he said, then headed for the door. "I'll speak to your doctors."

She launched herself off the bed and managed to get between him and the door. Her ankle throbbed with the effort. "You will not," she declared, trying not to wince at the pain. "I have no intention of being a burden on anybody, much less on someone I barely know."

"I don't think you have a choice," he said, his gaze unwavering.

"Of course there are choices," she insisted, even if most of them were impractical or unpalatable to someone who treasured her independence and didn't want to lose it even temporarily.

"Give me one."

"I'll go to a motel and hire a nurse," she said at once, grabbing at the first idea that came to her.

"Why waste that kind of money, when you can come with me? Do you have money to burn?"

"My homeowner's insurance will pay for the motel, and my medical coverage will pay for the nurse," she said triumphantly, praying it was true.

"And where will you find this motel room?" he asked.

"Miami's a tourist destination. There are hundreds of hotel rooms."

"And most of them are either packed with tourists willing to pay two or three hundred dollars a night or are filled up with insurance adjusters, fly-by-night contractors who've swarmed down here hoping to make a quick killing doing repairs or people just like you who've been displaced by the hurricane and who got there first."

Allie sighed. He was probably right. "Then I'll go into a treatment center. How bad can it be? I'll only be there a few days."

Ricky shrugged. "If that's what you want," he said mildly. "Institutional food. Antiseptic smells. A hard hospital bed. If you prefer that to my comfortable guest room and my mother's home-cooked meals, which I'm sure she'll insist on bringing over, then go for it."

He wasn't playing fair. This room was already closing in on her. She doubted a change to another medical facility would be an improvement. And she'd definitely had her fill of bland, tasteless meals. Cuban food was her very favorite. Her mouth watered just thinking about sweet, fried plantains.

But could she move in with a man who was virtually a stranger? Especially one who stirred her hormones in an extremely disconcerting way?

As if he sensed that she was wavering, he gave her an irrepressible grin. "I won't even try to seduce you, if that's what's on your mind."

"Of course that's not on my mind," she protested a little too vehemently, even as a guilty flush crept up her cheeks. "Don't be ridiculous."

His grin spread. "If you say so, *mi amiga.*"

*Friend?* she translated derisively. That's all she was to him? For a man she'd barely met forty-eight hours ago, it was actually quite a lot, but for reasons she probably shouldn't explore too closely, she found it vaguely insulting.

As if to contradict his own words, he lifted his hand and caressed her cheek, allowing his thumb to skim lightly, but all too sensually across her lips.

"Come on, Allie. A few days. It's a way out of here. That's what you want, isn't it?"

She swallowed hard. More than anything, she thought. More than anything, she wanted not just out of the hospital, but to go home with Enrique Wilder. The powerful yearning terrified her.

Not once in recent years had she given in to her own desires. She had become cautious and practical and self-protective. Heaven help her, without even realizing it, she had turned into her parents.

And two nights ago she had almost died. Maybe it was time she got back to living every single minute of every day.

"If you're absolutely sure that it won't be an inconvenience," she said finally, trying to ignore the wave of heat that continued to build simply from that light touch against her cheek. "And it's just for a few days."

His gaze locked with hers. "A few days," he echoed softly. He bent his head, his mouth hovering a scant inch above hers.

She yearned for him to close the distance, prayed for it, but he jerked away instead, his expression suddenly troubled.

"Sorry," he said roughly. "I'll go find the doctor."

And then he was gone.

*Sorry,* Allie thought, sinking gingerly to the side of the bed. He was *sorry* he'd almost kissed her. She was trembling inside, filled with anticipation, and he was *sorry?*

If she could have backed out of this deal of theirs right now, she would have, but he would have no trouble at all guessing why. It would be too humiliating.

She could keep this crazy lust under control for a few days, especially if he was gone most of the time as he'd promised. It was probably no more than some out-of-whack hormonal reaction to coming so close to dying. It probably had nothing to do with Enrique Wilder at all.

He walked back into her room just then, and her pulse ricocheted at the sight of him. Okay, she thought despondently, it had everything to do with him.

But she could control it. She had to.

"All taken care of," he announced. "Let's get you out of here and go home."

Just the mention of the word did her in. Two days of pent-up emotions crowded into her heart. Allie thought of her own home, unrecognizable now, and had to fight the sting of tears. Ricky regarded her with alarm.

"What's wrong?" he asked. "What did I say?"

Before she could respond, he gave a low moan and knelt in front of her, taking her hand in his. "Home? That's it, isn't it? I'm sorry. You'll rebuild, Allie."

"Of course," she said with sheer bravado. "It just caught me by surprise for a second, realizing that I don't actually have a home anymore."

"Well, for now you have a home with me," he reassured her.

The promise gave her comfort. It might be only a stop-gap solution, but it was enough for now. For the first time since the whole ordeal began, she didn't feel quite so terrified and alone.

## Chapter Four

Ricky wasn't sure exactly what had possessed him to insist on taking Allie home with him. He'd never in his life lived with a woman, had always assumed he wouldn't until he got married. He'd never been serious enough about any female to allow her into his world. A few had slept in his bed, but all had left the next morning, most never to return.

He protected his freedom with blunt words and clean breakups, when necessary. No woman had helped him decorate, not even his mother or sisters. From the color of the paint to the spread on the bed, he had chosen it all. It was a haphazard decor, because he'd made impulsive choices depending on what struck his fancy or what he'd been able to find when he'd had a few minutes to shop.

The house itself was small compared to the homes in the area where Allie had lived—two bedrooms, a living room and dining area, one bath and a kitchen that could best be described as cozy. He could stand in the middle and reach the stove, the refrigerator or the table without taking a step. He considered the setup efficient, when he thought about it at all.

The house might not be fancy, but it suited him, because the backyard was filled with trees—grapefruit, avocado, mango and orange. There was nothing better than walking outside first thing in the morning and plucking fresh fruit for his breakfast. Once he'd seen those trees, nothing else had mattered.

The fenced-in yard was also perfect for Shadow. On the first day Ricky brought him home, the shepherd had chosen a favorite spot in the shade, which he guarded as zealously as Ricky did his privacy. Eventually Shadow had allowed Ricky to put a lawn chair in the vicinity to share it. They spent a lot of relaxing hours out there, Shadow dreaming his doggie dreams about chasing squirrels, and Ricky sipping a beer and thinking about as little as possible.

How was Allie going to fit into their bachelor life? Surely in just a few days—which was all he'd bargained for—she wouldn't get any ideas about putting artificial flower arrangements all over the place or sweet-smelling soaps in the bathroom.

Suddenly an image of lacy underwear and panty hose hanging over his shower rod popped into his head. But rather than making him shudder, he found himself eagerly anticipating the intrusion. Did she wear skimpy little scraps of sexy lingerie or practical cotton panties? The speculation heated his blood by several degrees.

"Geez," he muttered under his breath. "Get a grip." He glanced over guiltily, relieved to see that her gaze was directed out the car window. Obviously he was losing it.

No, the truth was, he had lost it earlier, back at the hospital. When Allie had faced him in that faded hospital gown, looking battered and bruised and vulnerable, he hadn't been able to stop the invitation from crossing his lips. Even if he'd managed to keep silent initially, the impulse would eventually have overwhelmed him. He knew he could never in a million years have made himself walk out of that room without insisting on taking her along. The more she'd resisted, the more determined he had become. The woman got to him, no doubt about it.

Still, this wasn't a permanent living arrangement. It was only a temporary solution to an emergency, he reassured himself. It was nothing personal, though that didn't seem to stop his body from reacting predictably every time Allie so much as glanced his way. If he'd spotted her in one of the clubs on South Beach, he doubted he would have given her a second glance. She was too all-American, too petite for his taste. So why did he want her so badly? Because he'd mentally declared her off-limits the second he'd invited her into his home?

He felt a light tap on his shoulder, and his body jolted. He made himself turn, his gaze clashing briefly with troubled blue eyes.

"Are you really sure you want to do this?" she asked.

"I said I did, didn't I?" he said, grateful that she couldn't hear the tenseness in his voice.

"But you managed to get me sprung from the hospital. I'm sure I could manage on my own, if you wanted to drop me off."

"Where?" he asked testily, then cursed himself when he saw the quick rise of hurt in her eyes. There was the problem. She might not be able to detect the nuances of his voice, but she could obviously read his expression. And her every emotion was in her eyes, right there for even an insensitive jerk like him to see.

"I'm sorry," he apologized. "I shouldn't be reminding you that you don't have a home of your own."

"No, I'm the one who's sorry. You're being kind enough to do me a favor and I must seem incredibly ungrateful."

He reached for her hand, gave it a reassuring squeeze until they reached a red light and he could turn his head to face her so she could easily read his lips. "Allie, we're going to make this work, okay? Having you at my place is not going to be a problem," he lied, because to even hint otherwise would send her running and they both knew that, for now, she had no where else to go.

And, if he were being totally honest with himself, even if she had, he would have wanted her with him. The troubling question was why? Duty and obligation didn't seem to cover it. And any other possibility was unacceptable.

Allie desperately wanted to believe that Ricky meant what he said, because he was right—for the moment she had nowhere else to turn. She vowed, though, to cause as little disruption to his life as possible.

She had to admit to being curious about how a man like Enrique Wilder lived. He was all male, and she imagined that, despite his disclaimers earlier, he had his share of women. Would they have left their imprint on his home? Would his sisters have descended on the place to see that their baby brother had all the material comforts a man required?

She fought a smile as she realized that unless he had made a rushed phone call from the hospital, there had been no time for him to invite in a swarm of people to tidy up and ready the house for her arrival. His invitation had been too impulsive. She would be seeing exactly how Ricky lived, for better or for worse. The thought of tossed-aside shirts and damp towels on the bathroom floor, an atmosphere more male than any she had ever experienced, gave her an inexplicable little quiver of anticipation.

As Ricky turned onto a street in an older section of Coral Gables, Allie eagerly studied the neighborhood for clues about his personality. Small, modest homes sat cheek by jowl with brand-new mansions. She knew the area had strict rules for everything from setbacks to the color of paint that could be used, which somehow made the mix of old and new work.

She was relieved when Ricky pulled into the driveway of a stucco house with a tile roof and a lush front lawn, covered with a thick, green carpet of grass. Towering palms and dense shrubbery lined the walkway from the garage to the house. Bright-purple bougainvillea climbed up the sunlit walls of the garage. Other than a few stray branches and a littering of leaves, it didn't even look as if it had been touched by the hurricane. The landscaping seemed to have been in place for years, unlike her pitiful attempts to turn her yard into something more verdant than the small plots of green sod and one pin oak sapling the developer had considered sufficient for each property.

"It's lovely," she told Ricky, captivated by the effect.

When he would have led her inside, she stalled, peppering him with questions about the names of the various plants. To his credit, he not only knew, but responded with patience and increasing amusement.

"Allie, don't you think we could do this another time, perhaps when you're not in pain?" he finally asked. "I'll write it all down for you."

For a few minutes in her excitement she had actually forgotten about the pain and about the awkwardness of the circumstances. Now it all came flooding back.

"Sorry," she said, avoiding his gaze. "It's just that I love to garden and everything down here is so new to me. I'm still trying to figure out what works in this climate. Did you do this yourself?"

She had to make herself look at his mouth, so she could understand his response. Gazing at those sensual lips was not exactly a hardship, but she was beginning to realize that it was dangerous. The more she focused on his mouth, the more she wondered what it would feel like against her own.

Suddenly she realized she'd done it again, gotten lost in her own wicked thoughts, and had paid no attention to the words he was uttering.

"What?" she asked, an embarrassed flush climbing into her cheeks. "Could you say that again?"

"Am I talking too fast?"

"No, I just got distracted for a moment."

His eyes twinkled with knowing laughter. "Really? By what?"

She frowned at the teasing. "Never mind." She looked away.

He tucked a finger under her chin and turned her to face him. "I said that I did some of it. Fortunately, if you pick the right plants, the tropical climate takes care of the rest. Except for mowing the grass, I don't spend a lot of time worrying about upkeep."

"I imagine you don't have a lot of free time."

"No, and sometimes I can be gone for a couple of weeks at a stretch with virtually no notice."

"When there's an earthquake," she guessed.

"Or a flood. Any kind of natural disaster, really."

"I don't know how you do that. All that devastation and human suffering. It must be such sad work."

"Sometimes it is," he agreed. "But there are moments when we find a survivor against all the odds. That's what we have to focus on, the unexpected miracles."

He put his hand in the middle of her back and guided her up the walk. He unlocked the front door and opened it, then steadied her when a German shepherd bounded toward her. At a command from Ricky, the dog promptly sat, tail wagging as he stared up at her. Allie regarded the big dog warily.

Ricky caught her attention. "Allie, this is Shadow. He helped us to find you after the storm. Shadow, this is Allie. You remember her. Can you shake her hand?"

The dog raised his paw. Allie took it, then hunkered down to scratch the dog's ears. "Thank you, Shadow. I owe you."

"Offer him a doggie treat every now and then, and he'll be your pal forever," Ricky said. "I'll show you where I keep them. Just remember not to overdo it. He doesn't need one every time he looks pitiful and begs. It works on my nieces and nephews, so he tries pretty regularly.''

Allie chuckled. "I'll keep that in mind."

"Ready for a tour of the house?" Ricky asked. "It'll take about two minutes. Then, if you'd like to lie down for a while and rest, I'll try to come up with something for dinner."

"I've rested more than enough," Allie said. "I can help with dinner."

"Not tonight," he contradicted. "I promised the doctor you'd stay off that ankle as much as possible for the next couple of days."

Her gaze clashed with his. "You shouldn't make promises you can't keep."

"Oh, I think I could find some way to keep you in bed if I absolutely had to," he said.

His eyes smoldered in a way that made Allie swallow hard and look away. Surely he didn't mean... She met his gaze again. Oh, but he did. She could recognize the desire even without hearing the likely sensual undertone of his voice.

"About that tour," she said, all too aware that her voice probably sounded breathless.

He grinned. "Right this way."

From the moment they stepped into his living room, she knew that Ricky—and no one else—was responsible for the decor. The overstuffed sofa looked comfortable and very masculine. The leather recliner that faced the television sat next to a small table that was littered with newspapers.

The walls had been painted a bright yellow with white woodwork. One large, unframed oil painting hung on the wall behind the sofa, a scene of the Everglades at sunset with a vibrant poinciana tree in the foreground. The streaky orange shades of the sunset and the red blossoms of the tree were so vivid they seemed unreal, but Allie knew the artist had gotten it exactly right, because she had seen the setting herself. She stood in front of the painting, as awed by it as she had been by the real thing.

"It's magnificent."

"Thank you."

His vaguely embarrassed expression caught her attention more than the polite response. "You painted it?" she asked, astounded.

"Yes," he admitted with a diffident shrug.

"Ricky, it's amazing. Have you done others?"

"One or two. Nothing much."

"Why on earth not?"

"It's just dabbling," he protested.

Her gaze narrowed as she studied him. "I imagine someone told you that real men don't paint."

His lips quirked ever so slightly. "My father did express some concern about it."

"Then your father is an idiot."

He placed a hand over his heart in exaggerated shock. "Don't let my mother hear you say that."

"I'll say it to her or to him," she said fiercely.

"Allie, it's okay. It's not as if I grew up desperate to be an artist. I wasn't prevented from pursuing it. I paint when I have the time or inclination."

"You're wasting an incredible talent."

"I'm not. I love my career. I am exactly where I was meant to be with my life, doing something that really matters." He rubbed a thumb across her cheek. "Thanks for being so ready to defend me, though."

She restrained herself from arguing. Perhaps he *was* doing what he'd chosen to do with his life. After all, she barely knew him. She was in no position to judge his choices, to assume he was a firefighter because his father considered that more appropriate for a son than being a painter.

Maybe she had been so quick to do battle on his behalf because fate had taken her own choice away from her. Still, losing her music to fate was one thing—losing it to a domineering parent would have been quite another. Had she been in Ricky's position, she would have fought like anything to keep her music in her life.

As they completed the tour, she discovered a few more examples of his work in the other rooms of the house, all vibrant with color, all capturing scenes of the unspoiled Florida landscape. The paintings, even the small ones, dominated the rooms in which they were hung. Wisely, though, Allie kept from forcing another debate of the wisdom of his decision to relegate painting to the status of a hobby.

The guest room he showed her to was spotless and uncluttered. There was a small dresser and a comfortable bed with a dark-blue spread that picked up the exact shade of the tumultuous ocean in the painting that hung above the headboard.

"There should be room in the closet," he said, opening the door to demonstrate.

Allie managed a tremulous smile. "For what?" It was hard to believe that all she owned were the robe, underwear, sneakers, jeans and T-shirt Jane had bought and taken to the hospital.

Ricky looked disconcerted, then apologetic. "I'm sorry. I wasn't thinking. I'll put out a call to my sisters. They can bring you a few things or go shopping for you, whichever you'd like.''

She gestured toward the outfit she was wearing. ''As long as you have a washer and dryer, I can make do with this for a day or so. Then I'll go shopping.''

''Trust me, they all have clothes to spare, some no doubt with the price tags still on them. Maria and Elena are always battling their weight. They buy things too small, counting on them as an incentive to lose a few pounds. I'm sure they will be delighted to get them out of their closets, so the outfits no longer mock them for their failure.''

Allie chuckled, totally understanding their feminine logic. Ricky, however, was clearly mystified by it. ''Will you explain to them that you only want to relieve them of the clothes that are too small?'' she asked.

Ricky looked justly horrified by the suggestion. ''Are you crazy? I value my life too much to even hint at such a thing. Let me call, Allie. You'll feel better when you have some things of your own. A few days from now, next week, when you're feeling stronger and have your insurance money in hand, you can shop to your heart's content.''

Years of struggling for independence made her want to refuse, but common sense told her he was right. ''Thank you, but please, don't let them overdo it. One or two things will be plenty. The insurance adjuster promised to have an initial check for me by next week, so I won't have to rely on my credit cards to shop.''

He nodded approvingly. ''I'll call now, but I'll tell them not to come by until morning, when you've had a chance to settle in. Anything else you need—a favorite hand lotion, shampoo, cosmetics?''

''I have a few things from the hospital that will do for now.''

''You're sure?''

''Absolutely,'' she said, determined not to put him or his sisters to any more trouble than she already had. ''By the way, when you speak to them, how will you explain me?''

''You mean the fact that there's a beautiful woman living in my house who happens to be all but naked?''

''You can't say that,'' she protested, even as laughter bubbled up. She had a feeling he was scoundrel enough to make exactly that sort of outrageous remark.

''Of course I can,'' he said. ''Then again, that will bring them flying straight over, so I won't. I'll simply tell them the truth.''

''And what will they think?''

''That you must be an astonishing woman for me to break my rule.''

''What rule?'' she asked with a frown.

His solemn gaze locked with hers. ''Never to let a woman move in with me unless I intend to marry her.''

Allie had to struggle to keep him from seeing how shaken she was by his admission that he didn't make a habit of inviting women into his home to stay. Why her? she wondered.

Because he pitied her, of course. Nothing else. How *could* it be, when he hardly knew her. Still, she couldn't stop the feeling of disappointment that washed over her.

Ridiculous, she chided herself. This was a temporary haven. It had been offered as such, and what kind of idiot would she be to wish for anything more?

But she did, she admitted. She liked the lingering looks they'd shared, looks that sizzled with tension and promise. She liked the little shivers of anticipation that his unexpected touch sent through her. She liked the male scent of him, the hard feel of his muscles.

She simply liked Enrique Wilder, because for the first time in years, she felt completely and totally like a woman. Even if nothing more happened between them, even if all he offered from now on was a room and a roof over her head, he had given her an incredible gift. He had reminded her that she had lost her hearing years ago, not her life.

Until she'd met him, she had convinced herself that what she had was enough. That because her days were crammed full of activities, she was living. Now she knew better.

Because none of that had made her feel half as alive as one glance from her new roommate.

## Chapter Five

"Could you repeat that?" Maria asked when Ricky called and gave his oldest sister a shortened version of Allie's clothing predicament.

He should have known there was going to be trouble. "Which part of 'She needs clothes' didn't you understand?" he asked impatiently.

"Forget the clothes. I'm still on the part where you asked this total stranger to move in with you."

"Temporarily," he reminded her.

"She must be gorgeous."

He saw no point in denying the obvious, since his sister would see Allie for herself before another day was out. He thought of her pixie face, her untamed curls, the killer eyes. "She is, in an all-American way."

"Not your usual leggy brunette?"

He hadn't realized that his habits were so predictable that even his big sister knew his type. "No," he admitted.

"But you are attracted to her?"

"That's not the point."

"What is the point?"

"She's all alone with nowhere to go. I have room for her. It's not a big deal, Maria. I'd do the same for anyone."

"Did you happen to rescue anyone else the other day?"

Ricky saw exactly where she was heading with the question. "Yes," he replied warily. "But it wasn't the same. Most of those people had family."

"And Allie doesn't?"

His blood still boiled when he thought of her parents staying wherever the hell they were, rather than coming to be with her. "Not in Miami," he said tightly.

"Uh-oh," his sister muttered.

"Uh-oh what?"

"You've gone all protective, haven't you? I can hear it in your voice."

"What if I have? Somebody has to look out for her."

"You don't think you're carrying this hero-to-the-rescue tendency of yours a little too far?"

"No, I don't."

"How old is this woman?"

"I don't know. Twenty-nine, thirty, maybe."

"Ah," she said dryly. "An actual grown-up. And you don't think she can look out for herself?"

Ricky ignored the implication that he usually dated women who were less than mature. Instead, he tried to imagine how Allie would react to any suggestion that she couldn't manage on her own. He tempered his response accordingly. "Well, of course she could, but why should she have to, when I can pitch in for a little while?"

His sister muttered something in Spanish suggesting he was delusional, then added, "I'll be there in an hour."

"Not tonight," he countered. "In the morning. She's exhausted."

"There you go again, being protective of her."

"Doctor's orders," he contradicted, grateful to have them to fall back on. He could produce a list of very specific instructions if he had to. "He wants her to rest."

"Of course," Maria said with a laugh. "I wonder exactly how much rest she'll get in your bed."

"Dammit, Maria, she is not in my bed. She's in the guest room."

"For how long, I wonder?"

Ricky bit back a curse. "Maybe you should just stay away," he said. "I'll call one of my more understanding sisters."

"When it comes to speculating on your love life, *niño*, no one is more understanding than I am. I'll be there first thing in the morning."

"On good behavior," he instructed.

"I won't embarrass you," she promised.

"And you'll call the others?" he asked, not sure he was prepared to endure three more inquisitions, much less his mother's cross-examination once she got wind of Allie's presence. His mother would make this conversation with Maria seem like little more than idle chitchat.

"With pleasure," Maria said.

Ricky could all but see the grin spreading across her face. "Don't bring all of them in the morning," he warned. "Just a few clothes."

"Oh, Ricky, Ricky, Ricky," she chastised. "Do you really think I'll be able to keep any of them away?"

"Try," he pleaded. "Allie's not up to it."

"Allie or you?" she taunted.

"Both of us, okay. Just you, Maria, and I will be forever in your debt."

"Really?" she said, sounding suddenly more co-operative. "And in return for my help, you'll keep the boys for a weekend? All of them?"

He sighed, knowing what an incentive that would be for her to keep his other sisters away from his house. "I will," he agreed. "Two weekends if you can keep Mama away from here, as well."

Maria laughed. "Now, that, little brother, is beyond even my powers of persuasion. I'll have to settle for one weekend alone with my husband."

"At least try," he pleaded again. "I'll even go to Pedro's next three concerts."

Everyone in the family dreaded the concerts, because seven-year-old Pedro and his classmates had more enthusiasm than musical talent. The events were torture, and excuses not to attend inventive and widespread. And poor little Pedro was beginning to catch on. To have his heroic uncle Enrique attend would go a long way toward improving his status among his classmates. Maria knew it.

"I will convince Mama to stay home tomorrow if I have to tie her to a chair," she said with grim determination. "And the next concert is on Thursday. Plan to be there."

Ricky grimaced. "You do your part and I'll put it on my calendar," he promised without enthusiasm.

Satisfied that he had done what he could to keep Allie from being intimidated by a gathering of the Wilder females, he hung up and turned his attention to dinner. He had steaks in the freezer and plenty of vegetables for a salad. It wouldn't be fancy, but it would be filling. Allie needed to get her strength back, and he was going to need all of his to keep fending off his mother and sisters.

While Allie rested, he started the charcoal on the grill, defrosted the steaks in the microwave, then made the salad. He set the table on his patio and made sure the steaks were safely indoors and out of Shadow's reach. He'd learned his lesson the hard way. There wasn't a lot of human food the dog liked, but steak topped the list. Shadow could accomplish astonishing feats when there was a nice juicy slab of meat involved.

"Outside," he ordered the disappointed dog.

Shadow stood on the opposite side of the screen door, an expression of betrayal in his eyes.

"You're not going to make me feel guilty," Ricky added.

"Guilty about what?" Allie asked.

She had managed to slip into the kitchen without Ricky even being aware she was in the vicinity. He was going to have to remember that she moved so silently and watch what he said. Of course, unless she was right in front of him, he was safe enough, but it would be wise to remember it just on general principle.

"I thought you were sleeping," he said. "Wasn't the bed comfortable?"

"The bed was fine. And I did rest for an hour."

"Are you hungry?"

"Starved, actually. Everything they say about hospital food is true. It's tasteless. Wouldn't you think a place where the doctors keep telling you to eat to keep your strength up would do a better job of preparing something worth eating?"

"You would," he agreed. "Is steak okay? And I've fixed a salad."

"Perfect. What can I do to help?"

"That depends on what you'd like to drink? Iced tea? Coffee? Water? Beer?"

"Iced tea sounds wonderful. Shall I make it?"

Because she so obviously needed to make some sort of contribution, he pointed out the location of the teakettle and the tea bags. Unfortunately, the size of the kitchen all but guaranteed that they would keep bumping into each other as they moved around. Each brush of hip against hip, thigh against thigh made Ricky's blood sizzle. He was so aware of Allie, so blasted tempted to stop her in her tracks and kiss her that he finally grabbed the steaks and backed out the door.

"I'll be outside," he said. "Cooking."

She looked as relieved as he felt. "Will we eat out there?"

"Yes. The table's all set."

"I'll be out with the tea in a few minutes, then."

Ricky moved to the grill, closed his eyes and took a deep breath. It didn't calm the flutter of nerves at all. He couldn't imagine what was wrong with him. Women didn't make him nervous. In fact, he loved women. All women. He could flirt with the most intimidating female on earth without so much as a tingle of unease. He could dance slowly, sensually with the sexiest woman alive and experience no more than the expected stirring of arousal. So why was he acting like a love-struck teenager around Allie Matthews? Why was his body behaving as if he hadn't had sex for months?

Whatever the answer, Ricky was pretty sure he was going to hate it.

After Ricky went outside, Allie stood perfectly still and forced herself to draw in a deep, calming breath. No man had rattled her like that in years. Her only comfort was the fact that he had seemed as disturbed as she was.

"It's the situation," she muttered. "Of course we both feel a little awkward. He's apparently not used to having a woman underfoot, and I am definitely not used to bumping up against anyone so...*male* every time I turn around."

But what she felt wasn't awkwardness. Not exactly. What she felt was an edgy need, a hunger for something more than the whisper of his thigh against hers in a glancing contact that had lasted no longer than a heartbeat.

She had lost her virginity years ago, to a man she had thought herself in love with. Maybe she'd forgotten over time, but she couldn't recall that he had ever made her feel this wicked sense of anticipation, this unspoken awareness.

She had been nineteen when she had met Jared Yardley in one of her music classes. Only a few months later they'd had sex for the first time. She recalled feeling grown-up and vaguely thrilled by the decision that she was ready to take such a step. She didn't remember feeling much of anything during the act itself. Not that first time, which had been rushed and uncomfortable.

Nor any of the times after that, now that she thought about it. Once she'd lost her hearing and left school, they had broken up, and there had been no one in her life since. Living with the memory of that single experience of having a lover, she had assumed that was just the way sex was, and she couldn't imagine what all the hoopla was about. Now she was beginning to see that she might have gotten it all wrong.

If Ricky could make her feel hot and shivery at the same time with a casual touch, she had to wonder what he could do if he put his heart and soul into it.

She was so distracted by her speculation that she forgot to keep an eye on the teakettle. She was startled when Ricky came inside and stepped up to the stove to take the kettle off the burner.

"It was whistling," he explained, when she regarded him quizzically.

"Sorry. I wasn't paying attention. I usually watch for the steam."

"No problem."

"You can go back outside, if you want. I'll pour it over the tea bags."

"Trying to get rid of me, Allie?"

She swallowed hard at the teasing glint in his eyes. "Of course not. Why would I want to get rid of you?"

"I have a feeling I make you nervous. Do I?"

"Not you," she insisted. "The situation. I've never stayed with a man."

"Have you ever had roommates?"

"In college."

"Then think of this as the same thing."

She tried to compare living with Ricky to sharing space with the two giggling adolescents who'd been her freshman roommates. She shook her head. "Sorry, I don't think that's going to work."

"Why not?"

"Did you have roommates in college?"

"I didn't go away to college. I went right here in town. Later, though, I shared an apartment for a year."

"With a guy?"

He nodded.

"Was it the same as this?"

"Hardly," he said at once, then sighed. "Yeah, I see what you mean."

"So what are we going to do about it?" she asked, determined to discuss the situation sensibly and get it under control.

Ricky's expression turned thoughtful, then impish. "I do have one thought."

"Which is?"

He took a step closer, which had Allie instinctively backing toward the counter. He put a hand against the counter on either side of her, effectively trapping her.

"This," he said, lowering his head until his lips hovered just above hers.

Allie could feel the heat from his body reaching out to her. His breath fanned across her cheek. Anticipation stirred inside her as she waited and waited for him to close that infinitesimal distance.

When he did, when his mouth settled on hers, an amazing sense of calm and inevitability spread through her. The action was bold and unexpected, but the kiss itself was as light as the caress of a butterfly. It was unimaginably tender, shocking from a man who exuded such overwhelmingly masculine strength. Because it was so deliberately gentle it made her yearn, made her want things she had never imagined wanting, filled her with a sense of wonder.

Her pulse scrambled. Heat spread through her. And through it all there was the sensation of that wickedly persuasive mouth against hers, asking for more, hinting at everything but demanding nothing.

When he pulled back slowly, unwillingly, Allie uttered a harsh, "No," before she could stop herself. She felt his lips curve into a smile as they returned to hers for one more lingering caress.

She sighed when he abandoned her again, then avoided his gaze, until he captured her chin and gently forced her to face him.

"Better now?" he asked.

She blinked and tried to interpret the question. "Better?"

"Now that we've gotten that out of the way," he explained. "It was bound to happen sooner or later."

Was it? Allie hadn't guessed that when she'd agreed to move in temporarily. Hoped for it, maybe, but she assured herself she definitely hadn't grasped the inevitability of it.

"Because you can't go for more than a few hours without kissing a woman who's in close proximity," she said with what she hoped was just the right amount of teasing inflection.

Looking vaguely hurt by the question, he stepped away from her, leaving her feeling suddenly bereft.

"It won't happen again," he informed her, his expression serious and determined. "We'll just make sure not to come into the kitchen at the same time."

"Why?" she asked, before she could stop herself.

"Because I don't want you to think that I invited you here so I could take advantage of the situation." He ran a hand through his hair. "I thought it might relieve the tension to get the kiss out of the way. That was probably a mistake."

She could never bring herself to think of anything as wonderful as that kiss as a mistake. She studied him curiously. "Did it?"

"Did it what?"

"Relieve the tension for you?" It surely hadn't for her. If anything, she was more restless than ever, more anxious to know where a devastating kiss like that could lead.

Ricky looked shaken by the question. "Dammit, Allie, you don't ask much, do you? How can I answer that without causing you to run for the hills?"

"The truth might be a good place to start," she suggested.

He shook his head. "I don't think you're ready to hear the truth," he said, slamming through the back door and leaving her to stare after him.

She couldn't stop the smile that began at the corners of her mouth and spread. So, she thought with a touch of feminine satisfaction, it had gotten to him, too.

Knowing that made it a whole lot easier to pour the just-brewed tea into a pitcher, add a tray of ice cubes and carry it outside where she would have to face him. He was concentrating on the steaks with a frown knitting his forehead. She had a feeling that frown didn't have anything to do with worries over whether the meat was going to turn out rare or well-done.

He glanced up warily when she held out a glass of iced tea. "Thank you."

"You're welcome." She nodded toward the grill. "The steaks smell wonderful."

"They're almost done."

"Anything I can do?"

"Just have a seat," he said, then added pointedly, "over there."

Allie bit back a grin. Was he afraid she'd edge too close and distract him again? Maybe she should, but she wasn't bold enough for that. Instead, she dutifully settled into a chair at the round redwood picnic table, sat back and sipped her tea. Shadow came over to rest his head in her lap so she could scratch behind his ears. Or maybe he just meant to ingratiate himself in hopes of getting any leftover steak later.

"Did you speak to your sister?" she asked when Ricky eventually joined her at the table.

"Oh, yes," he said, his expression bland.

"Did she have a lot of questions?"

"My sister could put an investigative journalist to shame," he said, a grin tugging at his lips.

"Was she satisfied with your answers?"

"Temporarily," he admitted. "And she promised to hold off all the others for a day or two in exchange for me baby-sitting her sons for a weekend."

Allie laughed. "You bribed her?"

"You wanted peace and quiet, didn't you?"

"Not half as much as you did, apparently," she teased. "You don't think your sisters are going to make too much out of my presence here, do you?"

"Oh, yes," he said fervently. "You have no idea."

"Then I guess they'd better not catch us kissing," Allie said.

His frown returned. "There will be no more kissing," he declared with grim determination.

"Too bad," she said mildly, surprised at her own daring.

He carefully placed his fork on his plate and leaned toward her. "Allie, don't do this."

"Do what?" she asked innocently.

"Tempt me."

"Is that what I'm doing?" She truly hadn't been sure it was working. She was relieved to know it was.

"Blast it, you know you are," he said with evident frustration. "Stop it."

"Why?"

He blinked and stared. "Why what?"

"Why stop?"

"You know perfectly well that wasn't part of the deal."

"True," she agreed. "It's just a bonus."

"You don't have to feel obligated," he began.

Before he could continue, Allie felt something akin to fury begin to stir inside her. She wasn't totally familiar with the sensation, because she'd always been very slow to anger. Now it bubbled up, hot and urgent.

"Obligated," she said, her voice rising sufficiently to draw a warning *shush* from Ricky. She allowed her voice to climb one more decibel as she repeated the word.

Ricky winced.

"I do not feel *obligated* to do anything," she

snapped. "When you kissed me, I kissed you back because I wanted to, not because I felt *obligated.* Since when did that word have anything at all to do with me moving in here? Were you thinking that sooner or later I'd feel *obligated* to do more than exchange a few little kisses? Despite your earlier denials, is that what this invitation was really all about?"

Ricky rubbed his hand across his face. Clearly, he hadn't expected her to tear into him. "Look, that is not what I meant," he declared, his expression defensive. "Of course, you don't owe me anything for letting you stay here. There are no strings at all. None. That was exactly the point I was trying to make, when you got all hot under the collar. Maybe you misunderstood what I said."

"Maybe I couldn't hear you, but I could read your lips just fine. This isn't about me being deaf."

He winced. "No, of course it isn't. I'm sorry if I sounded as if I thought it was. It's just that there are going to be some adjustments here. We hardly know each other. There's bound to be some miscommunication. It doesn't have anything to do with whether or not you can hear."

Allie sighed. Perhaps she had overreacted...on that point, anyway. She did tend to get defensive occasionally when dealing with the hearing world.

"Maybe we should start over, establish some boundaries," she suggested.

"I thought that was what I was trying to do when I said there would be no more kissing," he said with evident frustration.

"I suppose that would be a good place to start,"

she said, hiding her reluctance to agree to any such thing.

Of course, despite the relief that spread across Ricky's face, she already had a pretty good sense that any such agreement was absolutely, positively doomed to failure.

## Chapter Six

Ricky had never been so relieved to get an emergency call in his life as he was when Allie was sitting right across from him, all but daring him to kiss her again.

Oh, she was saying all the right words, agreeing that there would be no more moments like that one in the kitchen when he'd discovered that she tasted better and was far more intoxicating than wine. But her eyes held a challenge. In fact, he was pretty sure that she was going to dare him to break their agreement before the bargain was even sealed.

And he would do it, too, because he wanted her, now more than ever. He'd convinced himself for about ten seconds that it was circumstances and proximity that had him aching with need, but he was pretty sure now that he knew better. It was Allie, pure and simple. Intentionally or not, she was going to drive him crazy.

So when his beeper went off, he all but bolted, not just from the backyard, but from the house. He kept right on going to the station even before he called on his cell phone to see what the emergency was. For all he knew, it could have been Tom wanting to sneak in a quick game of poker. It didn't matter, as long as it got him away from temptation.

As it turned out, the lieutenant had called them in on standby because of an imminent hurricane threat to the Louisiana Gulf Coast. That meant another long night of waiting, just in case there was devastation similar to what had happened in Miami. Normally the waiting made Ricky restless, but tonight the effect was compounded by the fact that he'd left Allie waiting for him at home.

He reached for the phone, then realized belatedly that he could hardly call. She wouldn't even know the phone was ringing. And he had no other way to get word to her about when he might get home again.

"Blast it," he muttered, slamming the receiver back into place. He tried to tell himself that he owed her nothing, but he simply couldn't leave her there to wonder what had become of him.

"What's wrong with you?" Tom asked, regarding him curiously. "Did you have to cancel a hot date?"

"No, it's Allie," he responded without thinking.

Tom's eyes lit up. "Allie, as in the beauty you plucked from the rubble the other day? What about her?"

Ricky had really hoped not to get into this with his partner. Tom would make way too much out of it, and Ricky would wind up as the butt of endless good-natured joking around the station. Not that the ribbing would be a new thing, but for some reason he didn't want Allie's name tossed around as if she were just another conquest.

"Never mind. It's nothing," he said. "I'll figure something out."

Tom regarded him with feigned hurt. "Who better to help than me, your buddy, your pal, the man you trust with your life?"

"You can't help. You're in the same boat I'm in, right here, waiting to sail, so to speak."

Tom straddled a bench and beckoned to Ricky. "Sit. Talk to me."

Ricky surmised his friend wasn't going to let the subject drop. With a sigh he sat. "Allie's at the house," he began.

"Your house?" Tom asked, eyes wide with shock.

"Yes, my house," he retorted impatiently. "Whose did you think I meant?"

"You could have meant your mother's."

Which probably would have been the smart place to take Allie from the outset, Ricky concluded. Neutral turf. Oh, his mother might have pestered him with questions, but at least his denials that Allie meant anything to him would have been more believable if she was staying with his family, rather than him.

It would also have made it more difficult for those sizzling kisses to lead them both into more dangerous territory. Under his mother's watchful gaze, he would have been lucky to steal a peck on the cheek.

Oh, well, he thought with a sigh. It was too late now.

Tom regarded him with approval. "So, the beautiful Allie is at your house. Very smooth, Enrique. Quick work.''

''She didn't have anyplace else to go,'' he said defensively. ''None of which is the point.''

Tom grinned, obviously enjoying Ricky's discomfort. ''Then explain the point. I'm all ears.''

''I left tonight before I knew we were going to be stuck here indefinitely. Now I don't have any way to get word to her.''

''You can't…'' He glanced toward the phone, then nodded with sudden understanding. ''Of course you can't.''

Since leaving her there wondering and worrying, particularly after the way he'd bolted, was completely unacceptable, Ricky concluded he had only one choice. ''Can you cover for me?'' he asked Tom. ''I'll run home, explain things and be back here in twenty minutes. We won't take off that fast, even if a call comes the second I'm out the door.''

For once Tom didn't indulge in his usual taunting. He just nodded. ''Go.''

''Thanks, pal. I owe you one. I'll be back in twenty minutes, tops.''

Ricky was halfway to the door before Tom hollered, ''Just don't hang around for any hanky-panky.''

''Allie and I are not engaging in any hanky-panky,'' Ricky retorted. *Not yet, anyway.*

He actually made it home in five minutes and was surprised to find most of the house in darkness except for a lamp in the living room. The remains of their dinner had been cleared away, the dishes washed. He headed down the hall to the guest room, then cursed when he saw the light was out. Allie was probably asleep and he was going to have to wake her, no doubt scaring her half to death in the process.

Leave her a note, a little voice murmured in his head. He acknowledged it might be the thoughtful, sensible thing to do for both their sakes, but that didn't seem to slow his progress toward her room.

He eased the door open and peeked inside. The instant the light from the hallway flooded into the room, Allie sat straight up in bed, her eyes wide with alarm.

"Ricky?"

He flipped on the overhead light, then stepped inside so she could see his face. "Sorry," he said, chagrined. "I didn't know whether to wake you or not. I'm going to be stuck at the station for hours and I might have to go out of town. I couldn't think of any other way to let you know."

He tried not to notice that her tousled hair was skimming shoulders that were bare as she clutched the sheet to her breasts. Sweet heaven, the woman was naked. His imagination seized on that and stripped away the sheet before he could get a tight rein on it. Fortunately her gaze was locked on his face, so perhaps she didn't notice the unmistakable sign of his arousal behind the zipper of his suddenly uncomfortable jeans.

"A hurricane?" she guessed. "The one heading for Louisiana?"

"Exactly."

"I saw the news reports. Is there anything you want me to do for you here if you have to go? Shadow…?"

"He'll stay with me. Just keep an eye on things," he said. "Make yourself at home. And don't forget that Maria is coming in the morning. She has a key, so don't be startled if she just walks in. She knows you won't hear her knock.''

She nodded. "I'll be waiting for her."

He dragged his gaze away and took a step back. "I'd better go. Good night, Allie."

"Good night. Stay safe."

He turned off the light and carefully shut the door, then leaned against the opposite wall and waited for his pulse to stop racing. He was in trouble here. Big trouble.

All the way back to the station he thought of her last words to him. *Stay safe.* She had said it as if she actually might worry about him. When was the last time someone had done that? Oh, of course his family worried, but they'd had years to get used to his comings and goings, to accept the risks he took. Allie was the first woman he'd allowed to get close enough to be affected by his well-being, the first one he'd left behind to worry.

He told himself not to let that matter. If his mind was on Allie at all, he could lose concentration on whatever job had to be done. That would put not only his life but Tom's at risk, to say nothing of whatever victim they might be attempting to rescue.

He had to forget all about her, block her from his mind, and that was that. Unfortunately, as he'd already discovered in a few brief days, that particular feat was going to be easier said than done.

Allie had stayed awake for a long time after Ricky left. She'd been stunned the night before, not by him walking into her room, but by his thoughtful return to let her know that he might have to leave town.

She doubted he was used to being accountable to anyone.

She was sitting at the kitchen table, stirring sugar into her coffee, when she glanced up and saw a beautiful, dark-haired, dark-eyed woman surveying her intently. The family resemblance would have been unmistakable even if she hadn't seen a photograph of all the Wilders the night before.

"Hello," she said tentatively. "Maria?"

A grin identical to Ricky's spread across the woman's face. "And you must be Allie. I hope I didn't scare you. I tried not to sneak up on you."

"Unfortunately, having people sneak up on me is pretty much a given in my life. At least my heart doesn't leap out of my chest anymore."

Maria chuckled, then sobered as she stared longingly at the pot of coffee. "Thank goodness. Can I have some of that? We were running late this morning at my house and I left to take the kids to school before I could get my first cup."

Since she was already reaching into the cupboard for a mug, Allie concluded she didn't really expect a response. Because she knew what it was like to need a jolt of caffeine to feel civilized, she waited as the other woman poured the coffee, stirred in three heaping teaspoons of sugar, then took her first sip.

"Ah, heaven," Maria murmured, her expression content. She glanced around. "So, where's my brother?"

"He was called in to work last night. He thought he might have to go to Louisiana."

"He left you all alone on your first night here?"

Allie grinned at her apparent indignation. "He

does have a job. I doubt his boss would care that he has a temporary houseguest.''

Maria's gaze narrowed. ''Then this is only temporary?''

''Of course. He just offered to let me stay here so I could get out of the hospital. The doctors wouldn't release me until I knew where I was going and had someone around who could make sure I rested. Your brother took pity on me. As soon as I make other arrangements, I'll be moving out.''

Maria laid her hand on Allie's. ''Do me a personal favor, okay? Don't be too quick to go.''

Allie regarded her with confusion. ''Why?''

''My brother might not admit it, but he needs someone in his life.''

''But what makes you think *I* should be that someone? You don't really know me. He doesn't, either, for that matter.''

''He invited you to stay here. That alone tells me quite a lot. As for me, you can spend the next hour satisfying my curiosity.''

''Oh?'' Allie said cautiously.

''I want to know everything about you, all the deep, dark secrets, all the hopes and dreams.''

Startled by Maria's unrepentant determination to dig into her life, Allie fell silent.

''Uh-oh, I've come on too strong, haven't I?'' Maria said. ''Sorry. It's big-sister syndrome. I usually don't get this much privacy with Ricky's women, so my curiosity is never satisfied. It's very frustrating. I suppose it doesn't really matter, because they're usually gone in no time at all.''

She smiled warmly. ''Something tells me, though, that you have staying power.''

Allie was stunned by the assessment. How could Maria come to such a conclusion based on a meeting that hadn't even gone on for fifteen minutes yet?

"Sisterly instinct?" she asked.

"Exactly. You're beautiful. You're vulnerable."

When Allie would have protested, Maria held up her hand. "Maybe not typically and not for long, but for the moment you definitely require a little extra pampering, a certain amount of macho protectiveness." Her smile turned smug. "And you are in his house. I rest my case." She took a mock bow.

Allie chuckled. "Very confident, aren't you?"

"Very." Her smile faltered. "Unless you're not interested in him. You do find our Enrique attractive, don't you?"

"I'd have to be blind, as well as deaf, not to find him attractive," Allie admitted without hesitation. "Beyond that…?" She shrugged. She was not going to bring up those kisses. She was not even going to think about those kisses, much less discuss them with his sister.

"It's a start," Maria declared with evident satisfaction. "Now then, do you want to take a look at the clothes I brought along? I stopped short of raiding my sisters' closets, so what you're getting comes from mine. It was easier than trying to explain to them why they couldn't come along this morning. Ricky was afraid that you would find all four of us at once to be overwhelming."

"Are the others like you?" Allie asked.

Maria chuckled. "I like to think they're worse, but yes, pretty much."

"I can't wait to meet them, then," Allie said honestly. "But Ricky was right. All of you at once would have been a little terrifying."

Maria regarded her with understanding. "Your whole world must seem a little off-kilter now. I can't imagine going to bed in a home, with belongings that you treasure, and then waking up to discover that everything, including the house, has been destroyed. Was anything at all salvageable?"

"To tell you the truth, I don't know. I came here straight from the hospital, so I haven't been able to go back and sift through the debris to see if anything's left."

"Would you like to do that now?" Maria offered. "I could take you. You might feel better if you could find some things of your own."

Allie desperately wanted to take her up on the offer, but she knew she wasn't strong enough physically for the ordeal. "I'm afraid I don't have the stamina just yet. And my ankle and knee are still in pretty bad shape."

"Of course. What was I thinking?" Maria apologized. "You let me know whenever you're ready. If Ricky doesn't have time to take you, I will. Or the family and I can go for you."

"I couldn't ask you to do that. You've already done too much."

"I've taken a few things out of my closet. What's the big deal? To tell you the truth, I'm glad to be rid of them. I bought them too small and they're mocking me."

Allie tried unsuccessfully to hide a grin.

"I see Ricky told you about my habit of deluding myself when it comes to my weight," Maria said. "A woman in this family has no secrets. Well, no matter, you will put them to good use, so there was a reason I bought them, wasn't there?''

''Before we look at the clothes, could you do me a favor? I'd like to let my former neighbor know where I am. Otherwise, she'll waste a trip to the hospital.''

''Give me the number and I'll call right now.''

Once the call to Jane was made and Maria had managed to satisfy her elderly neighbor that Allie was in good hands, Ricky's sister took her into the guest room. To Allie's amazement she found a huge pile of clothes on the bed. There were shorts, slacks, blouses and dresses, all still tagged an optimistic size eight.

''I know,'' Marie said ruefully when she saw Allie examining a tag. ''These hips haven't been in a size eight in ten years, but I can dream, can't I?'' She surveyed Allie. ''Will they be too big for you?''

''No, perfect, I imagine. I'll choose one or two to get by with—''

''Don't be ridiculous. Keep them all. If there are any you don't want, give them back later.''

''Then let me pay you, at least.''

''Absolutely not. They might not even be to your taste. The important thing is that they'll do in a pinch.''

''I insist on paying you for anything I keep,'' Allie repeated firmly. ''That's only fair. Then you can buy something else.''

''Whatever,'' Maria said dismissively, sifting through the stack until she hit on a bright-blue sundress. ''Try this. It will be gorgeous on you. Very sexy.''

Because she'd never had anyone to go on shopping excursions with her and had always envied the fun it would be to try on clothes and giggle over the ones that looked absurd or get advice on the ones that looked best, she reached for the dress.

It wasn't her style. It was too revealing by far, but the color would be nice with her eyes, she thought, as she stripped to her underwear and slid the dress over her head.

It fit like a dream. She could tell even before she turned to look in the mirror. The silky fabric fell like a whisper to caress her thighs before ending just above her knees. It clung to her breasts, barely held in place by spaghetti straps.

Her gaze shifted in search of Maria's reflection in the mirror only to find Ricky's stunned face instead. She could see the muscles in his neck work as he swallowed hard. Her own mouth went dry and she pivoted slowly to face him.

"I was just..."

"You look..."

She grinned, anxious to know what he had been about to say. "You first."

"Amazing," he said, his gaze still riveted. "You look amazing. That dress was made for you."

"I don't really have anyplace to wear it."

"Sure you do," he contradicted. "We have a date to go dancing, remember?"

She was surprised that he remembered the promise he'd made when she was so terrified that she might be paralyzed. "I thought you'd probably forgotten all about that."

"I never forget an invitation to hold a gorgeous woman in my arms."

They were both startled when Maria waved a hand

between them to get their attention. "I'll just be going now," she said, barely containing her laughter as she added, "As if either of you will care."

"I heard that," Ricky said, his gaze returning to Allie.

Allie felt her skin begin to burn under the intensity of his scrutiny.

"You're back," she said, then winced at the statement of the obvious.

His eyes twinkled. "I am."

"You didn't have to leave town?"

He shook his head. "The storm weakened and veered back out to sea. Unless it strengthens and turns again, Louisiana should be in the clear. Then we'll have to wait to see about Texas or Mexico."

"That's great."

He blinked, then tore his gaze away. "I'm going to take a shower. Did you have breakfast?"

"Yes, but I can make you something."

He shook his head. "I ate at the station."

Allie nodded, feeling yesterday's awkwardness stealing through her again. What would he normally do with the rest of his day? She didn't want to interfere with whatever plans he might have made.

"Look, you do whatever you want to do. I'll probably go out back and read for a while, then take a nap."

"In that dress?" he inquired, his expression amused.

She glanced down, stunned to see that she was still wearing the sundress. "Of course not. I'll change." She gestured toward the pile of clothes. "Your sister got carried away."

"So I see."

Fumbling a little as she tried to untangle the hangers, she began putting the clothes in the closet without even examining them. A moment later she felt a tap on her shoulder.

"Yes?" She faced Ricky. Hands jammed in his pockets, he looked uncomfortable.

"Want to go somewhere for lunch?" he asked. "If you're not too tired."

She nodded. "That would be nice."

"I have to go to my nephew's soccer game after that. You can come along if you're up to it, or I can bring you back here."

Allie desperately wanted to go along, to feel as if she were becoming a part of this huge extended family of his, but the fact was she stilled tired easily.

"Can we play that by ear?"

"Absolutely."

Then he was gone and she was left clutching an armload of clothes. Her decision to stay here was getting more complicated by the second. The undeniable heat between them, his sister's generosity, a lifelong yearning for boisterous siblings and close family ties, it was all too alluring. She was very much afraid she might start wanting something that wasn't in the cards.

But years ago she had vowed never to let fear control her life. This experience might be totally unexpected, it might come to a painful conclusion, but in the meantime, she was going to savor every second of it.

## Chapter Seven

Ricky took an icy shower to cool down enough to face Allie again. That dress his sister had brought over ought to be banned…except in the privacy of his home. He wouldn't mind seeing Allie in it night and day. It was only a sundress, nothing fancy, but it did devastating things with her already potent eyes, drew attention to every dip and curve of her body, revealing way too much satiny skin in the process. He'd promised to take her dancing so she could wear it, but he already hated the prospect of other men ogling her.

When he went looking for her after his shower, he was relieved to find that she'd changed, though the white shorts and T-shirt she had on now weren't much of an improvement. She still looked way too tempting. Apparently his displeasure was evident, because she frowned when she saw the way he was studying her.

"Is everything okay?"

"Fine," he said tersely. "Are you ready to go?"

"Whenever you are," she said at once.

He gestured toward the door, then followed her out, trying to keep his gaze focused on something other than the sway of those slender hips and the bare expanse of shapely thighs. At this rate he was going to have to start buying his jeans in a larger size.

"Any preferences for lunch?" he asked when they were in the car.

"It's up to you. Whatever works with your plans."

"Are you always so agreeable?" he inquired irritably.

Her gaze seared him. "I thought I was being considerate," she said stiffly. "If there's a problem, I can stay here."

Ricky sighed. "Absolutely not. The only problem is me. I'm tired and cranky and taking it out on you."

"Maybe you'd rather take a nap than go to lunch," she suggested as if he were an irritable toddler.

Ricky ground his teeth together. "We're going to lunch," he insisted, glad she couldn't hear his tone of voice, which was less than gracious. "I know the perfect spot. It's guaranteed to put me in a better mood."

She gave him a wry look. "Then by all means, let's go there."

Even as he drove across the Rickenbacker Causeway, Ricky could feel the tension slipping away. With the sky a brilliant blue and the water of both

Biscayne Bay and the Atlantic sparkling, it was hard to think about anything other than how lucky he was to live in such a place.

He glanced at Allie and saw that she, too, looked more relaxed as she studied the narrow strip of palm-tree-lined beach and the water beyond. He tapped her arm, drawing her attention.

"Can't beat the view, can you? Look back toward the city," he suggested, indicating the Miami skyline over his left shoulder.

Allie nodded. "I know. It's my favorite drive. I come to Key Biscayne almost every weekend."

"Have you been to the restaurant in the state park?"

"The one at the lighthouse?"

He shook his head. "The other one."

Her expression brightened. "I didn't know there was another one."

"You'll love the setting," he promised.

A few minutes later, after driving through the small village of Key Biscayne, with its stretch of oceanfront condos and hotels on one side and mansions on the other, they reached the state park at the tip of the island. Ricky paid the admission, then made a right turn that took them to an inlet referred to as No-Name Harbor.

Built on stilts so that it sat above the water was a small, no-frills restaurant with an outdoor deck that faced back toward the southwest. The view was best at sunset, but even at midday it was like being on an isolated island, rather than just minutes from downtown Miami. A few boats bobbed at anchor in the harbor and a few diners sat with beers and fresh fish, enjoying the mild breeze that offered relief from the steamy early-October heat.

"Like it?" he asked Allie.

"It's wonderful," she said.

"A little rustic, but the fish is fabulous. You have the feeling they just threw in a line and caught it about the same time you placed an order."

Once they'd ordered their own fish sandwiches and drinks—a soda for her, a beer for him—he sat back with a sigh. A moment later he felt Allie's gaze on him. She gave him a slow smile.

"You look better already," she said.

"I feel better. Sorry about before."

"Want to tell me why you were so uptight?"

"Not especially."

"It did have something to do with me, though, didn't it? Ricky, if our arrangement isn't working for you, just say so. I can find someplace to go. I don't want to take advantage of an impetuous offer you'd rather you hadn't made."

"It's not that," he protested. "I just hadn't counted on..."

"Yes? Talk to me. We have to be able to communicate."

Her gaze was so trusting, so expectant, that he knew he'd never be able to lie to her face just to save them both a little awkwardness. "Okay, you want the honest-to-goodness truth?"

"Of course."

He thought of half a dozen ways to put it before finally settling for being blunt. "I'm attracted to you."

To his astonishment, she feigned an exaggerated sigh of relief.

"Thank goodness," she said. "I was worried it was my imagination."

"It's not funny, Allie."

She placed her hand on top of his. "Ricky, we're both adults. I'm not going to jump in bed with a man just because I'm attracted to him, but that doesn't mean I'm not going to admit the obvious."

His gaze narrowed. "Which is?"

"That I'm attracted to you, too."

He wasn't sure whether he was relieved or appalled by her admission. It definitely made things more complicated.

"I just want you to know that I'm not going to do anything to take advantage of the situation," he said.

Amusement flickered in her eyes. "Good, because I wouldn't let you even if you tried."

She said it with absolute confidence, as if she had loads of experience protecting herself from men like him. Ricky doubted that she did, but he had to admire her faith in her own values. Or maybe it was a lack of faith in his powers of persuasion.

He seized the hand that had been resting atop his. "Careful, angel. Some men might consider that to be a challenge."

"Are you one of them?" she asked, clearly more curious than fearful.

"On occasion," he admitted. "I've rarely been one to turn down a dare."

To his amazement her lips curved into a slow, provocative smile. "Then it will be very interesting to see how you handle this one, won't it?"

He groaned at the blatant taunt. Every time he turned around, Allie Matthews was surprising him.

Something told him that for the first time in his life he had met his match.

Allie watched the play of expressions on Ricky's face and took a great deal of satisfaction from clearly having stunned him. She knew she was playing with fire, but she also trusted him more than anyone she'd ever known. He had said he wouldn't take advantage of their situation, and she believed him. That gave her the freedom to test her powers of seduction.

She studied Ricky's now-wary expression and congratulated herself. So far she seemed to be quite good at it.

It also seemed like a smart time to scale back the game. "Which nephew is playing soccer this afternoon?"

Ricky stared at her blankly. "What?"

"I was asking about the soccer game. Is it one of Maria's sons who's playing?"

He nodded. "Tomás. He's actually quite good."

"How old is he?"

"Six."

"They have a soccer league for six-year-olds?"

"They do indeed. Of course, the kids are a little older before the game actually resembles real soccer, but they have a great time, and they're very enthusiastic. My brother-in-law coaches."

"Why not you?"

He grinned. "I coached for one week, but I kept forgetting they were only six. My competitive spirit kicked in and I put way too much pressure on them. After the first game my sister threatened to ban me from the stands as well as the sidelines. We compromised. I can sit in the stands, but I have to keep my mouth shut. Maria sits next to me to make sure I don't forget. I'm pretty sure she and her husband have a bet on how long my silence will last.''

Allie chuckled. ''Who's betting on you?''

''No one,'' he admitted, his expression rueful. ''The only question seems to be when, not if, I will break my promise.'' He studied her. ''How are you feeling? Do you think you'll be up to stopping by? Your color is better today.''

''I feel better,'' she admitted. ''But I don't know if I can last a whole game, and I don't want you to have to leave before it's over.''

''Haven't you been listening? You'll probably be doing everyone a favor if you get me away from there. You will earn Maria's undying gratitude, to say nothing of little Tomás's.''

''Then I'd love to go,'' she said, looking forward to seeing Maria again and to meeting her family. ''Will the other boys be there?''

''Absolutely, though they're usually running around and getting into mischief.''

A half hour later, Ricky pulled into a parking lot beside a soccer field. The game was apparently already under way, because the attention of the adults in the stands was riveted on the field.

As Allie and Ricky walked in that direction, three dark-haired boys, who seemed to range in age from seven or eight down to three or four, spotted him and raced in their direction.

''Guess what?'' the oldest one shouted, his face flushed with excitement. ''Tomás scored a goal, all by himself.''

''Only because the goalie ran off the field to go to the bathroom,'' his younger brother countered.

Ricky laughed. "That does make it easier," he said, then turned to Allie. "At six, the finer points of waiting for substitutions or time-outs seems to elude them."

"I can imagine," she said dryly. It would drive a particularly competitive coach to distraction. "Glad you're not coaching?"

"Glad I'm not coaching the other side, anyway."

The littlest boy was tugging on his hand. "Uncle Ricky. Uncle Ricky."

"What is it, *niño?*" he asked, scooping the boy into his arms.

The child pointed at Allie. "Who's she? Is she the one everybody's talking about?"

Allie was a bit disconcerted to discover that she'd been the topic of conversation in the family, but Ricky didn't seem the least bit surprised.

"Yes, she is," he told his nephew. "This is my friend, Allie Matthews. Allie, this little munchkin here is Miguel. His big brother is Pedro. Pedro is a budding musician."

Pedro politely extended a hand. "Hello."

Allie regarded him with immediate interest. "What kind of music do you like?"

"I play the violin," he told her shyly.

"I used to play the violin, too," she told him, aware that Ricky was staring at her with surprise that swiftly changed to sympathy as he realized the full implications of the revelation. "In fact, until I lost my hearing, I was going to be a music major. Sometimes I even played with a symphony orchestra."

Pedro's eyes widened. "Wow, that is so cool. How come you didn't tell us that, Uncle Ricky?"

"Because until just now I didn't know it."

Allie felt a tug on her arm and looked down into an upturned face.

"I'm a big brother, too," the remaining boy protested. "I'm Ramón, but my friends call me Ray. I'm five."

Allie grinned. "I'm glad to meet you, too, Ray."

"Is it true you were almost buried alive?" Pedro asked, clearly fascinated by the gruesome prospect.

Allie couldn't prevent the shudder that washed over her.

Ricky winced. "Sorry," he said to her, giving her hand a squeeze. He turned to his nephew. "Pedro, you don't ask people a question like that."

"But Mama said—"

"I don't care what your mother said. It's not polite to ask about something that would be very upsetting if it were true. Would you want to talk about it if you'd been trapped in a building that collapsed?"

Of course, a seven-year-old couldn't really imagine exactly how dire a circumstance that might be. Pedro's expression turned thoughtful, then decisive. "I think it would be cool."

"It would not be cool," his uncle declared.

"But you rescued her, didn't you? She's okay, and that makes you a hero. All my friends are talking about you. I can't wait till you come to my concert on Thursday so they can all meet you."

"Enough," Ricky said, ending the discussion, clearly embarrassed by the talk of his heroics.

"It's okay," Allie said. She smiled at Pedro. "I can imagine it must seem pretty exciting, but believe me, it wasn't. It was scary until your uncle came along. He really is a hero."

"I knew it!" Pedro shouted exuberantly, and went

racing off, no doubt to repeat the story. Miguel and Ray scrambled to keep up with him.

"Obviously you've made a conquest," Ricky told her. "Why didn't you tell me about your music before?"

"It never came up," she said with a shrug. "Besides, I try not to think about it too much."

"I'm sorry. Losing something you loved like that, something you'd intended to spend your life doing, must have been as hard as losing your hearing."

"It was," she said in a way that she hoped would end the topic.

Ricky took the hint and led the way to the stands. Allie noticed quite a lot of speculative looks aimed in their direction as they climbed up to join Maria. Ricky tried to maneuver Allie toward the space next to his sister, but Maria shook her head.

"Oh, no, you don't, Enrique. You sit next to me so I can clamp a hand over that big mouth of yours, if you forget yourself." She regarded Allie apologetically. "It's not that I wouldn't rather have you beside me."

"I understand," Allie said with a grin. "Completely."

"He told you, then, about his abominable behavior."

"He swears he has reformed," Allie confided.

"Ha! That I will believe when I see it."

"Okay, when you two have finished having your fun, I'd like to concentrate on the game," Ricky said.

Maria clucked disapprovingly. "It is the concentrating that is the start of the trouble. We are here for fun. That is all."

"There is nothing wrong with wanting to win," he countered defensively.

"Only when you wish to win at all costs. Now behave. You are making a bad impression on Allie."

He scowled at his sister. "And that would matter to you because…?"

"Because I like her," she said, winking at Allie.

Ricky draped an arm across Allie's shoulders. "I like her, too," he said, his gaze locked with Allie's.

"At last, something we can agree on," Maria said.

The warm acceptance of Maria and the flash of lust in Ricky's eyes combined to make Allie feel as if she had stumbled into her heart's desire. This was what she had always craved—the teasing, the sense of belonging. If the hurricane had been her worst nightmare, this…this was her dream.

She sighed. Ricky instantly cupped her chin and studied her face.

"Everything okay? Are you too hot? Tired? Would you like something to drink? There are sodas available."

The barrage of solicitous questions made her smile. "I'm okay. Stop worrying. I'll tell you if I need something or if I want to go."

She caught the smirk of satisfaction on Maria's face and had to resist the urge to return it with a smug grin of her own.

"So, Enrique," Maria began, her expression suddenly innocent. "Will you and Allie be coming to Mama's for dinner tomorrow?"

Allie held her breath as she waited for him to reply. Was he ready to subject himself to the speculation of the rest of his family? Was she, for that matter?

"What do you think, Allie?" he asked, his expression neutral.

"I think it's up to you. This is your family. Maybe we should discuss it when we get home."

He brightened at the reprieve. "Good idea."

"Well, I hope you'll be there, Allie," Maria said. "Everyone else is dying to meet you."

"I can just imagine," Ricky murmured, his voice apparently too low for his sister to hear, because she didn't react.

Allie, however, grinned. "Maria might not have heard that," she said. "But I did."

"It's not bad enough that I have a mother who, I swear, has eyes in the back of her head? I have to meet a woman who can read my mind?"

"It wasn't your mind," she said. "It was your lips."

"Whatever," he said miserably. "I'm doomed."

Maria, her eyes full of mischief, turned in their direction. "Yes, little brother, I think maybe you are."

In the end Allie opted not to go to the Wilders' for dinner. Ricky swore that he wanted her to come if she felt up to it, but she was beginning to sense that he was totally bewildered by how quickly things were happening between them. The truth was, she was no less confused. She concluded that a day apart would be good for both of them.

"But you'll be all alone," he protested.

"Not if you'll call Jane and give her a ride over here."

She couldn't deny that he had seemed relieved by the compromise. And Jane had been ecstatic at the idea of getting an afternoon away from her sister. She had arrived with a picnic hamper packed with food.

"But I'd planned to fix something," Allie protested when she saw it.

"You need to rest more than you need to be standing over a stove. Besides, it's not much."

Allie had to laugh as she began removing the contents of the hamper. Her former neighbor's idea of "not much" consisted of fried chicken, potato salad, coleslaw and a homemade key-lime pie, which she knew was Allie's favorite.

"Well, I see you're not going to starve," Ricky said, studying the food with obvious envy. "Maybe I could…"

"Stay," Jane invited. "There's plenty of food and I have a few questions I'd like to ask you."

He regarded her warily. "About?"

"Your intentions toward our girl, for starters."

He cast a frantic look at Allie, then backed up. "I can get those questions at my mother's."

Jane gave him an unrepentant look. "And she'll probably let you brush her off, won't she?"

"Hopefully," he agreed, then dropped a kiss on her cheek.

"Well, I'm made of tougher stuff, young man. You can get off the hook today, but I'll be watching you."

Allie laughed at his horrified expression. "She will be, too."

"I don't doubt it," Ricky said. "I'll be back in plenty of time to drive you home, Jane. Don't even think about calling a taxi or taking the bus."

She chuckled. "Are you kidding? When I'll have

the whole drive home to ask you all those tricky questions I've been storing up?''

"On second thought, maybe I should leave cab fare,'' Ricky countered.

"Too late now,'' Allie told him as she walked with him to the door. "Have fun with your family.''

"You have fun with Jane. I'll be back soon.''

After he'd gone, she turned to find Jane studying her. "You're falling for him, aren't you?'' her friend asked worriedly.

"Only a little,'' Allie admitted.

"Be careful,'' Jane warned. "That one has the devil in his eyes.''

"But the heart of an angel,'' Allie reminded her. "And the arms of a hero.''

"Oh, baby,'' Jane said. "Don't go mixing up heroics with love.''

"I didn't say anything about love,'' Allie insisted.

"You didn't have to say it. It's written all over your face.''

If that was true, Allie could only pray that Ricky wasn't nearly as adept at reading people as Jane was.

## Chapter Eight

By midweek, Allie was going stir-crazy. She desperately wanted to get back to work, but both Rick and her doctor were vehemently opposed to the idea.

"I promise I'll stay off my feet," she said while both men regarded her with skepticism at the conclusion of her follow-up appointment on Wednesday. She scowled at them and repeated, "I will."

"Not good enough," the doctor said, then glanced at Ricky. "See that she stays at home at least through the weekend. After that I suppose it won't hurt for her to go back part-time." His gaze shifted to her. "A half day, is that clear?"

The restriction grated even worse than his attitude. "I teach sign language, for goodness sakes, not aerobics. I can hardly wear myself out doing that."

"You teach kids, correct?" Ricky asked.

"Yes."

He glanced at the doctor. "Have you ever known kids to sit still?"

"Not mine," the doctor said.

"Not the ones I know, either," Ricky said.

"Well, my students are very well behaved," she argued. Judging from the look the two men exchanged, she was wasting her breath. "Never mind."

She walked out of the office without another word. By the time she reached Ricky's car, she was steaming.

"You do know that this is none of your business, don't you?" she said as she got in the car and slammed the door.

He didn't seem to be overly impressed by the reminder.

"Want to go to lunch?" he asked as he settled behind the wheel. Clearly he had no intention of getting into the fight she was itching to have.

"No, I do not want to go to lunch. I want to go to work. My students need me. It's disruptive for them to adjust to someone new."

"Sorry. You heard the doctor. Not till next week."

"You sold me out. You know I'm well enough to go back."

"Hey, it wasn't my call," he said, feigning innocence. "That's why they have follow-up visits, so the doctor can decide what the patient is capable of doing."

"I could have talked him into it, if you'd kept your big mouth shut."

"Doubtful," he said. "Now, about lunch…?"

"Forget lunch," she all but shouted. "You won't be able to stop me if I decide to go back tomorrow."

"How will you get there? Your car is still in the

shop. So are a zillion others, waiting to see if they can be repaired. I figure you're pretty much at my mercy for the time being.''

''I can rent a car or take a taxi, if necessary. And you can't watch me every minute. Sooner or later you'll have to go to work.''

He beamed at her. ''Actually, unless there's a natural disaster somewhere, I have the rest of the week off.''

That didn't please her nearly as much as it might have a couple of days ago. He seemed to be intent on seeing to it that she didn't do anything the least bit taxing. Ever since he'd taken Jane home on Sunday, he'd devoted himself to hovering. He was worse than her parents had been when she'd lost her hearing.

Maybe if there had been anything the least bit lustful in his attention, she would have been pleased, but he'd been treating her like a sister, and a pretty mindless sister at that.

She stared at him and noted the unrelenting set to his jaw. Okay, then, if that was the way he wanted to play it, she had an idea of a sneaky way to get even.

''As long as we're out, there is something I need to do,'' she began innocently.

''Name it,'' he said at once, clearly relieved to have the topic of work tabled for the moment.

''Shopping. I want to pick up a few things.''

''Clothes? Makeup? What?''

''All of it,'' she said, watching with amusement as the enthusiasm drained out of his face. He was such a man. By the time she finished with him, he would regret his part in keeping her away from her job. In fact, he might take her straight to the clinic and leave her there.

"What about all that stuff Maria brought?"

"She was very generous, but there are still things I need."

"Fine," he said, his expression grim. "We'll go to the mall, but just for an hour, Allie. That's all I'll agree to. You shouldn't be on your feet any longer than that."

"An hour will be just fine," she said, beaming at him.

Once he'd parked and they'd walked inside the mall, she aimed directly for a lingerie shop. Let him sweat, she thought triumphantly when she caught his pained expression. He was clearly torn between whether to accompany her inside or find a bench a safe distance away.

"Coming?" she inquired pleasantly, making absolutely sure he understood it was a dare.

"Sure." He trailed along reluctantly.

He stood amid the racks of lacy bras and bikini panties looking as terrified as if she'd just left him to fend for himself in a nursery of screaming babies.

Allie grinned at the twenty-something sales clerk, who couldn't seem to stop herself from casting surreptitious glances at Allie's very male companion. She turned her back on him finally and said in what was probably an undertone, "How'd you ever get him in here? Most men won't come near this place."

"Bodyguard," Allie confided. "He can't leave my side."

The young woman's eyes widened. "Oh, wow. I don't know what he's protecting you from, but I'd risk it to have him around day and night."

Allie raised her voice. "Trust me, honey, it's not nearly as much fun as you'd think."

Her words had the desired effect. Ricky's head snapped around in her direction just as she held up two pairs of bikini panties and inquired of him, "Which do you think?"

A dull red flush climbed his cheeks, but then his gaze locked with hers and it was as if he could read her mind. She could tell the precise instant when he figured out what she was up to.

"Why not try them on and model them for me?" he suggested. He reached out to a selection of lacy bras on a nearby display, sifted through them and plucked out a handful. "These, too."

Check and checkmate, Allie thought with a sigh. She wasn't nearly daring enough to take him up on the taunt.

"I'll take them all," she told the clerk, handing over the two pairs of panties, along with several other pairs that were less provocative. Then she sorted through the selection of bras Ricky had grabbed and chose three of those. She tried not to notice that he'd somehow gotten the size exactly right.

She moved to the counter to pay for the purchases, but a prickling sensation on the back of her neck told her that Ricky had followed. She glanced up into twinkling brown eyes.

"These, too," he told the clerk as he handed her a matching bra and panties in black lace. "But I'm paying for them."

Allie swallowed hard at the challenging glint in his eyes, but just as she was about to protest, he said mildly, "Save your breath, *querida.*"

As she watched in dismay, he glanced around at

the displays, wandered over to an extremely skimpy negligee in turquoise and brought that back to add to the pile. He winked at Allie. "I can't wait to see the color on you."

The clerk seemed oblivious to Allie's increasingly irritated reaction. She was too busy ringing up the additional sale.

"Thank you," she chirped as they left. "Come back again."

"Not in this lifetime," Allie muttered.

Ricky grinned. "Something wrong?"

"Not a thing," she snapped.

"You got what you went in there for, didn't you?"

And more, she thought darkly.

"Anything else you wanted to get while we're here?" he inquired cheerfully.

"No, I think I'm finished."

"Good, because I'm starving. All that shopping worked up an appetite."

His gaze locked with hers in a way that made her feel as if steam must be rising from her skin.

"How about you? Hungry?" he asked, though it was plain that food was the last thing he craved. "Or would you rather go home and go to bed?"

Allie very nearly choked. "Excuse me?" she said, when she could catch her breath.

"I was just asking if you were too tired to stop for lunch," he said, not even attempting to fight the grin that was slowly spreading across his face.

"Lunch sounds good," she said.

And the first thing she was going to do was order a huge glass of iced tea for her suddenly parched throat. Of course, if she were smart, she probably ought to get a pitcher of ice water and dump it right

over her head. Maybe that would chill her steamy
thoughts and clearly overheated hormones. It would
also serve as a harsh reminder not to play provocative games with a man who understood the rules far
better than she did.

Ricky should have been feeling very smug, but
instead he was all hot and bothered, and it was his
own blasted fault. He might have been the victor in
that little game in the lingerie store, but Allie was
definitely having the last laugh.

She was seated across from him in the restaurant
looking thoroughly cool and collected, while all he
could think about was getting her home and into—
and then out of—those sexy little numbers he'd pur-
chased. Definitely bad planning on his part, since he
had made her a promise that things were going to
remain strictly platonic between them. He was going
to honor that promise or die trying, which he was
fairly sure was a distinct possibility.

He tapped her hand to get her attention, then gestured toward the menu. "What are you having?"

"I feel like something spicy," she said slowly, her
gaze lingering on his mouth. "What about you?"

Ricky had a hard time getting his brain to kick
into gear.

"There should be plenty of jalapeños in the *que-
sadilla*," he said finally, pretending that he hadn't
even noticed the deliberately suggestive note in her
voice. "Want to share that as an appetizer?"

"Sure."

"What else?"

"I'd say a cheeseburger, but I don't think I could
eat a whole one," she said.

"We'll split that, too."

"Will that be enough for you?"

"Absolutely," he said. "Especially if we have dessert."

"You're on your own there," she said. "With all this inactivity, I don't dare."

He could think of one way to burn off a few calories, but he resisted the urge to mention it, even in jest. He wasn't even supposed to be thinking about such things. Of course, that was a little like telling a jury to ignore inflammatory testimony after they'd already heard it. After telling himself to keep his thoughts on the straight and narrow where Allie was concerned, erotic images taunted him nonstop. He forced his attention back to the matter of their lunch.

"We'll see how you feel after the burger," he said, then beckoned for the waitress and placed the order.

After the waitress had gone, he realized Allie was studying him. "What?" he asked.

"Can I ask you something?"

He nodded, though the expression on her face made him a little wary.

"You don't subscribe to the idea that if you save someone's life, you're responsible for it, do you?"

"Of course not," he said without hesitation.

"Then why are you being so protective where I'm concerned?"

He tried to shrug it off. "Habit, I suppose. I always tried to look after my sisters. That's just the way I was brought up. My father ingrained it into my head that it was a man's job to protect the women in his life—mother, wife, sisters, whatever."

Her gaze remained doubtful. ''And that's all it is?''

Ricky was no more convinced of the honesty of his answer than she was, but he didn't want to admit that it could be anything else. He certainly wasn't about to tell her he'd never before felt this need to watch over a woman, to protect her—even from himself. What he felt around Allie was a far cry from anything he'd ever felt for the women in his family. Maybe because protectiveness and jealousy and lust were somehow getting all mixed up together.

''Of course,'' he said, lying brazenly. ''What else could it be?''

She shrugged. ''I have no idea, but it's a relief that that's all it is, because then I don't feel quite so bad telling you that I find it extremely annoying.''

He'd gotten that earlier, back in the doctor's office and later in the car. ''So I gathered.''

''Then you don't care that I find your attitude irritating?''

''Not if it gets the job done,'' he said. ''Talk to me again in a week, when you're back on your feet. Maybe you'll be able to convince me to back off.''

''I *am* back on my feet now.''

''To some degree,'' he acknowledged. ''But if I weren't around, you'd be pushing yourself to do too much. You'd be back at work and hunting for a place to live and wearing yourself to a frazzle worrying about Jane and all your other neighbors.''

''How can you say that? You barely know me.''

''I know enough. And what I didn't figure out on my own, Jane explained.''

Indignation set off sparks in her eyes. ''The two of you are in cahoots?'' she asked.

"You bet. And before you ask, I've also spoken to your boss. I got the skinny from Gina, too. You're an overachiever, Allie Matthews. That's a very admirable trait under most circumstances, but under these—" He shrugged. "Let's just say I've decided to save you from yourself."

"You had no right to run around behind my back, prying into my life."

"Sure I did."

She scowled at him. "How can you say that?"

"Somebody had to." He patted her hand consolingly. "It could have been worse."

"I don't see how."

"I could have brought in the big guns."

She regarded him in confusion. "Big guns? What does that mean?"

"I could have put my mother on the job. You'd still be flat on your back in bed and watching soap operas in Spanish."

A chuckle erupted before she could stop herself. Ricky grinned.

"Have I made my point?" he asked.

"Oh, yes," she said.

"You are in my debt," he added, heaping it on.

"Apparently so."

He leaned forward. "So, what do I get for my trouble?"

Allie was clearly struggling with herself. She moistened her lips, started to lean forward as if to meet him halfway, then sat back with a heavy sigh.

"I'll have to think about it," she said.

He winked at her. "Let me know if you can't come up with anything, because I have a few ideas myself."

"Yes," she murmured. "I imagine you do."

"Great ideas," he emphasized, keeping his gaze firmly fixed on her mouth, even as he told himself he was being a louse…again. The flirting was as ingrained in him as breathing. He couldn't seem to stop himself.

Allie didn't so much as bat an eye. Rather she met his gaze boldly and directly. "Care to elaborate?"

"Oh, I think it will be a whole lot more fun if we both just rely on our imaginations."

"Something tells me yours has been in overdrive," she said wryly.

"Since the moment we met," he conceded. "Since the moment we met."

By the time they got home and Allie had gone to her room for a nap, Ricky was in such a state of arousal he changed clothes and went outside to mow the lawn, hoping to exhaust himself before he had to see Allie again over dinner.

He was hot and sweaty and covered with grass clippings when he heard the slam of a car door. He moaned as he considered the possibilities. Whoever it was, he didn't want to see them.

"Hey, Enrique, you out back?" Tom shouted as he rounded the side of the house clutching a six-pack of beer.

Ricky assured himself that his receptiveness increased only because of that beer. He nabbed one before his friend could settle on the chaise lounge next to his.

"You're a mess," Tom said after a casual survey. "How do you expect to land the fair maiden looking like that?"

"Actually, I'm hoping to look and smell so disgusting, she won't come within a foot of me," he said.

"How come?"

"Because she's dangerous," he said before he thought to censor himself.

"Dangerous how? Is she sleepwalking with a butcher knife or something?"

"Hardly."

"What then?"

"She just exists, that's all," he grumbled, taking a deep swallow of the cold, refreshing beer.

"Oh, boy," Tom said with a hoot. "You have it bad, my friend."

"I do not."

"Of course you do. You have gone way beyond just scheming to get her into your bed, haven't you?"

Ricky scowled at the suggestion. "Don't be ridiculous. I don't do the happily-ever-after thing. You know that."

"It's not so bad. Maybe you should consider it."

If Tom had suggested they both take up skydiving, Ricky couldn't have been any more stunned. "This from a man who bolted from a marriage practically before the ink was dry on the license."

"*I* didn't bolt. *She* did. And we're talking about you, not me."

Despite the denial, Ricky thought he detected something wistful in his friend's expression. "Is there something going on with you and Nikki? Have you seen her?"

"Last night," Tom admitted grudgingly.

"Intentionally or did you bump into her someplace?"

"No, I stopped by."

"Really?" Ricky barely hid his surprise. He thought they hadn't seen or spoken to each other in months, despite his mother's attempts to push them back together. "And?"

"And nothing."

"Nothing happened? She kicked you out? What?"

"We talked for maybe five, ten minutes. Then her date showed up."

"Geez, I'm sorry, *amigo*."

"The man was wearing a pin-striped suit, for Pete's sake," Tom continued. "He's an accountant, you know, for one of those muckety-muck firms. A real nine-to-fiver. How boring is that?" He tried valiantly to achieve an air of disdain, but his hurt was evident.

"I'm sorry," Ricky said again. "Do you think it's serious?"

"Hey, he's exactly what she says she's always wanted."

"But did it look serious?" Ricky persisted. "Sparks flying, that kind of thing?"

"What difference does it make? If this jerk is what she thinks she wants, she'll find a way to talk herself into having a relationship with him."

"Then you'll just have to find a way to talk her back out of it," Ricky told him. "You know anybody with a better gift of gab than you? Present company excluded, of course."

Tom seemed to take heart from the reminder. "Hell, no," he declared.

"Well, then, if you want her back, fight for her. Do you want her back?"

Tom's expression turned miserable again. "I can't be a damned desk jockey, not even for her."

"Maybe there's a compromise."

"Such as?"

"I don't know. That would be up to the two of you."

"Well, if one exists, I can't think what it is," Tom said. "Let's talk about you and the beautiful Allie instead. Where is she?"

"Napping."

"She's in bed and you're out here? You are slipping."

"Go suck an egg," Ricky grumbled.

"Is that the response of a mature man?" Tom taunted.

"No, it is the response of a man who's at the end of his rope. I say I go in and take a shower, and you and I go out on the town. How about it?"

"Fine by me. I got nothing better to do."

"Good. That's settled then." A night on the town would prove to him that he wasn't really hooked on Allie. He'd probably find a dozen other women before the night was out who'd be more gorgeous, more willing, and less vulnerable. Leggy brunettes with sultry smiles.

Unfortunately, when he stepped inside the back door, he found Allie bending over in front of the oven. The view was too alluring to ignore. He enjoyed it for a full, uninterrupted minute, and every thought of leggy brunettes fled.

When she finally stood up and caught sight of him, she jumped, clearly startled.

"Sorry," he apologized, his voice husky.

"I didn't know you'd come in."

"I keep forgetting about sneaking up on you. What's in the oven?"

"Dinner. I found a roast in the freezer. I made pot roast."

He frowned. "I thought you were resting."

She scowled right back at him. "I was and now I'm not."

"You should have said something. Tom's here. We were going out."

If she was disappointed, she hid it well. "Fine."

"If I'd known you were cooking, I would have told you," he said, feeling defensive.

"It's not a problem. I'll have some of this tonight. You can eat the leftovers whenever you feel like it."

He didn't like it that she was letting him off the hook so easily, as if what he did didn't matter two hoots to her. "I suppose we could eat first and then go out," he said grudgingly. "Is there enough for Tom?"

"There's enough for an army, but don't stay on my account. I should have checked with you first."

"We'll stay," he said at once, wondering what Tom was going to make of the sudden turnaround.

"Fine. I'll set another place. Should I go out and tell him or will you?"

"I'll do it," Ricky said. If his friend was going to start laughing when he learned of the change in plans, Ricky didn't want Allie to wonder why. "How long till we eat?"

"A half hour."

"Perfect. I'll tell Tom, then take a shower and change."

Tom's reaction wasn't exactly what Ricky had anticipated. "Pot roast?" he echoed, staring longingly toward the back door. "The real thing. Not a frozen dinner?"

"The real thing."

"Damn, buddy, if you don't marry this woman, I might."

Ricky scowled. "Not in a hundred million years," he said fiercely.

Tom feigned shock. "Are you warning me off?"

"Isn't that what it sounded like?" Ricky retorted. "If not, I must be slipping."

"Message received," Tom said dutifully, but his eyes were full of mischievous sparks.

Ricky had the distinct impression he'd better take that shower and get back to the kitchen in record time. He wasn't quite sure whether he needed to be there to protect Allie...or his own interests.

## Chapter Nine

Aside from Ricky's vigilance, the only thing that kept Allie from returning to work on Thursday was the unexpected arrival of her boss from the speech and hearing clinic, first thing in the morning.

Looking smug, Ricky ushered Gina Dayton into the kitchen while Allie was sullenly sipping her third cup of coffee and glowering over the top of the paper. She felt her spirits improve the instant she spotted the energetic woman who ran the clinic.

"Gina, I had no idea you were coming," Allie said, signing for the woman's benefit.

Gina had been born deaf, but she had never considered it a detriment to achieving her dreams. She had been a grade-A student in high school, had graduated from college at the top of her class and had started her own cutting-edge clinic in her hometown of Miami. With her energy and her boundless optimism, she was a role model to her clients and her staff.

"Your friend called me last night and told me you were getting restless," she said, gesturing toward Ricky. "He seemed to think the only way to keep you at home would be to get you an update on your students. I decided to come in person."

"I'll leave you two to catch up," Ricky said, after surveying the scene with apparent satisfaction.

Allie reluctantly met his gaze. "Thank you."

"No problem. Enjoy yourselves. Gina, would you like some coffee before I go?"

Gina signed her response, clearly startling Ricky.

"Gina doesn't speak," Allie told him, "except with sign language. She said she'd get her own coffee if you'd point her in the right direction."

"But I spoke to her on the phone," he said.

Gina grinned and signed a response. Allie translated for him. "She says you actually spoke to her assistant, who acted as an interpreter for her."

"So the words were hers, but the voice was her assistant's?"

Allie nodded. "Exactly."

"But Gina reads lips?"

Gina tapped his arm, grinning. "I do."

Ricky gave her one of his devastating smile. "Okay, then. The coffee's over there. And I picked up some guava pastries this morning."

Gina's expression turned rapturous as she signed, "Heaven."

Ricky grinned. "I think I got that. Let me know if you need anything."

As soon as he was gone, Gina regarded Allie with obvious fascination. "Girl, what have you landed yourself in? The man is a certifiable hunk. And he's the one who rescued you? How did you end up living with him? No wonder you didn't want to stay at my place with a man like him waiting in the wings to take you in.'' Her fingers flew as she signed the barrage of questions.

"He's not bad," Allie responded cautiously.

"Are you blind, too?" the other woman inquired, patting one hand over her heart. "My pulse is still racing."

"Because you don't get out enough," Allie told her. "You work all the time."

"So do you," Gina responded. "Let me know if you decide not to keep him."

Allie wanted to explain that he wasn't hers to keep, but she couldn't quite bring herself to do it. Ricky might not be hers, but she couldn't see herself handing him over to another woman, especially someone she knew. Just the thought of bumping into him with someone else made her stomach churn.

She frowned at her friend. "You're married and the mother of a new baby."

"But I have friends," she said fervently. "They would be in my debt forever if I brought a man like Ricky to them. I was very impressed when he called the other day to express his concern about you. And when he called back to arrange this visit, I knew I had to get a good look at him for myself."

Even though Allie said nothing, Gina apparently got the message. "Hands off, huh? Okay. But if you spot any more like him, let me know."

"Will do," Allie promised. "Now tell me what's happening at the clinic."

"Your patients all miss you like crazy. They sent

cards,'' Gina said, drawing a stack of brightly col-
ored pictures from her briefcase.

Allie accepted them, but the first one of a little
girl's face with a tear on the cheek brought such a
lump to her throat that she put them aside to study
later, when she was alone.

"They love you," Gina signed, then gave Allie's
hand a squeeze. "We are all grateful that you weren't
hurt any worse than you were, and we can't wait for
you to get back."

"I could come in tomorrow," Allie said eagerly.

Gina held up protesting hands. "Not on your life.
I've already been warned by your friend in there that
you are not coming back till Monday. Period."

"Ricky Wilder does not run my life."

"But he has your best interests at heart. Listen to
him." She grinned. "Besides, if a man that gorgeous
offered me an incentive to stay around the house, you
can bet I wouldn't budge."

"That's what you say because you have a
choice," Allie complained. "He's not giving me any
choice at all."

"It's a few more days," Gina reminded her. "This
ordeal has been a shock. It's not just the physical
injuries you must deal with, but the emotional harm
it did. Have you even been back to your house?"

Allie shook her head. Even at the risk that looters
would take anything salvageable, she wasn't ready
to face it yet.

"You must go," Gina told her. "Put it behind
you. You know better than most the importance of
moving on."

The allusion to the weeks during which she'd
raged about her loss of hearing, rather than accepting

the reality, brought that whole, awful, wasted time back to her. "I know you're right, but I'm afraid memories of the hurricane will overwhelm me. It was terrifying."

"Have you thought of talking to a psychologist about it?"

"No. I'm coping. It will get better with time."

"And if it doesn't?"

"Then I will see someone. I promise."

Gina stayed for a few more minutes, sharing gossip about the staff, reporting triumphs of the patients. "We need to talk about Kimi Foley," she said referring to one of Allie's more troubling cases. "She's not doing as well as we'd like, but we'll discuss that when you come in on Monday."

She eventually plucked a few articles and reports from her briefcase and passed them along.

"Reading material," she said. "And some paperwork. But don't do any more than you feel up to."

"Thank you," Allie said fervently. Maybe she wouldn't feel so cut off, so completely useless, if she could at least do a little of the endless paperwork her job entailed.

She walked Gina to the door, gave her a hug, then stood watching her drive away, unable to hide the wistfulness she was feeling.

She felt Ricky slip up beside her. He draped a comforting arm across her shoulders.

When she glanced up to meet his understanding gaze, he reminded her, "Only a few more days."

She sighed. "I know."

But it seemed as if she'd already been stranded in limbo forever.

\* \* \*

With Allie settled more happily at the kitchen table with her paperwork, Ricky congratulated himself on the brilliance of his idea to get Gina Dayton to drop by.

After casting one last look at her, he stripped off his shirt and went outside to try to tame some of the shrubbery that was threatening to take over the front lawn.

He was hard at work, when he sensed he wasn't alone. Allie was sitting on the front stoop, arms around her legs, chin resting on her knees. She looked totally downcast again. He set aside his clippers and dropped down next to her.

"I didn't mean to distract you," she said.

"Then what did you mean to do?" he teased. "Get an eyeful of the scenery?" He deliberately glanced down at his gleaming chest.

Allie reacted with predictable embarrassment. "Of course not. I was just…" Her voice trailed off.

"Restless again?" he inquired sympathetically.

"Not exactly." She met his gaze. "I've been thinking."

"About?" he prodded when she didn't continue.

"I think I need to go back to my house."

He stared at her incredulously. "What? No way!"

"I have to do it. Your sister mentioned it the other day and today Gina brought it up."

He shot to his feet and began to pace. "They're both nuts," he declared. "Why would they suggest something like that?"

He felt Allie snag his hand and pull him to a stop, her expression frustrated.

"What?" she demanded.

He repeated what he'd said, then added flatly, "It's not a good idea."

"I think it is," she said with a determined jut to her chin. "Maybe some of my things can be salvaged. And even if they can't, I have to deal with what happened that night. I have to face it and move on. Will you take me?"

He struggled with the wisdom of what she was suggesting and his own fear that she wasn't ready to face that night. "Allie, I don't know."

"I'll find some other way to get there, if you don't."

He knew she would do it, too. Unlike the idle threats she'd made about sneaking back to work behind his back, he sensed that this time she'd made up her mind. She would go with him or without him. There was no way he would let her face it alone.

"I'll take you," he finally conceded. "When?"

"Now," she said with grim determination. She stood up to emphasize her declaration.

Ricky sighed. "Okay, now it is. Just give me a minute to clean up and put on a shirt."

"It's not like we're going someplace fancy," she protested. "We'll probably get filthy."

"Give me a minute," he insisted.

Inside, he made a quick, desperate call to Jane. "Do you think she's up to this?"

"If she says she is, you don't have a choice. I'll meet you there," the elderly woman said decisively.

"Want me to pick you up on our way?" Ricky offered.

"No, then she'll know you called. It'll be better if I just show up."

"Thanks, Jane. You're an angel."

"You can buy us both lunch when this is over. I have a craving for a nice, thick pastrami on rye with some kosher pickles."

"You've got it," Ricky promised. "See you soon."

To allow time for Jane to make her way back to her old neighborhood via public transportation, Ricky opted for a shower, rather than the quick cleanup he'd intended. He took his own sweet time about drying his hair and getting dressed, then shaved, too. By the time he went outside, Allie was prowling the yard impatiently.

"It took you long enough," she grumbled.

"Is that the thanks I get for making myself beautiful?" He leaned in close. "See, I even smell good."

A reluctant grin tugged at her lips as she sniffed his aftershave. "Very nice. Something tells me it's going to be wasted on the vermin likely to be crawling over the remains of the neighborhood, though."

"As long as it's not wasted on you," he said agreeably and headed south.

The closer they got to Allie's old neighborhood, the more her anxiety increased. She had knotted her hands so tightly in her lap that the knuckles had turned white and there were lines of tension around her mouth. Ricky made the turn off Dixie Highway, then pulled into the parking lot of what had once been a small strip mall. Now the roof was gone, and the few remaining windows were covered with graffiti-decorated boards. He put his hand over Allie's.

"You okay? We don't have to do this now."

"Yes, we do," she said tightly. "Right now. Just keep going."

The deeper they drove into the area, the more devastation they saw. At first only trees were down, with the occasional boarded-over windows, but then house after house began showing signs of being ravaged by what was now presumed to have been a hurricane-spawned tornado.

"Oh, God," Allie murmured, a hand covering her mouth, her eyes stricken. "I'd forgotten. Where you live, it's like the storm never happened, so I told myself it couldn't have been as bad as I'd remembered." Her devastated gaze met his. "But it is. It's worse, in fact. There's nothing left."

"We're turning back," Ricky said, reaching a decision. He couldn't bear the pain in her eyes.

"No, please. Let's just get it over with."

He hesitated, but the unyielding expression on her face never wavered. "Okay, fine," he said and turned onto her street.

The only way to be sure which house was Allie's was to count the piles of rubble from the corner. When he pulled to a stop, her dismayed gasp quickly gave way to a sob.

"Oh, baby," he whispered, reaching for her. He pulled her into his arms and let her cry, helpless to think of anything more he could do to comfort her.

He held her until a tap on the car window startled him. He glanced out to find Jane studying them anxiously. Her flushed complexion worried him. He beckoned to her to get into the back seat so she'd be out of the heat.

Allie shifted, staring in surprise when the door opened and Jane climbed in. Jane took one look at Allie's ravaged face and managed to lean over the seat to give her a comforting hug.

"It's worse the first time you see it," she consoled her. "Then you just have to start thinking about how exciting it will be to have a brand-new home where the old one stood."

Allie's wounded expression didn't brighten at all at the prospect.

"Why don't you two stay here in the air-conditioning?" Ricky suggested. "Let me rummage around and see if I can find anything worth keeping."

"I'll come, too," Allie said at once.

Jane exchanged a look with Ricky, then clasped Allie's hand. "Stay here with me for just a bit. It was terribly hot out there. I need a few minutes in this cool air."

Allie immediately regarded her with concern. "Are you okay? Would you like something to drink? I brought along some cold, bottled water."

"That would be wonderful," Jane said.

Ricky seized the opportunity to slip out of the car. He wasn't especially hopeful that he would locate anything of value in the debris, but it would probably be less stressful for Allie not to have to sift through things she had once loved that were now broken or caked with mud.

It was a thankless task. He found a photo album, but water had all but destroyed the pictures inside. He put it aside on the chance that one or two photos could be saved. He discovered a jewelry box, but even before he pried open the lid, he knew that anything valuable had been taken by looters. Inside, he found an old Sunday School attendance pin and a high school ring, but whatever else Allie had owned was gone.

As he sifted through the debris, he found the occasional shoe—but never its mate—a few unchipped dishes, a cast-iron skillet and an assortment of stainless steel knives, forks and spoons. He found one drape relatively unscathed, but the other in tatters. Sofas, chairs, her television were completely ruined.

He had just picked up a teddy bear, its fabric caked with dried mud, one eye missing, when Allie joined him. She reached for the bear with fingers that trembled, then hugged him to her as tears streaked silently down her cheeks.

"He'll look better when he's had a bath," Ricky said optimistically. "And I'm pretty sure Maria can replace the eye. The boys were always destroying their stuffed animals, then sobbing till she patched them up again."

"I got this bear when I was in the hospital when I lost my hearing," she said, her voice choked. "Brownie and I have been through a lot together."

"And you've both survived," Ricky reminded her.

"A little the worse for wear," she said, tenderly smoothing the bear's mud-caked tummy. She shook her head. "I don't know what I expected, but it wasn't this."

"You weren't exactly in any condition to check out the scenery when we got you out the other day," he reminded her. "You were in shock."

"Yes, I suppose I was." She visibly struggled to pull herself together. "Have you found anything else?"

"I put a few things over here," he said, showing her.

She held it together until she saw the photo album,

but then her shoulders shook with sobs. "It's like losing my entire past, as if it never existed."

"Don't be silly," Jane said briskly, stepping in when Ricky couldn't find a single word of consolation to utter. "They were just pictures. The memories are in your heart. You'll never lose those. And I imagine some of those pictures were taken by other people who very well might still have the negatives. We'll call your parents, some of your old friends, and put the album back together again."

Allie gave her a watery smile. "Thank you."

"For what?" Jane said dismissively. "I haven't done a thing."

"You came over here today. I know it wasn't an accident. Ricky called you, didn't he?"

"He might have mentioned you were thinking of heading over here," Jane conceded. "You should have told me yourself."

"It was an impulsive decision. Not a very good one, either."

"You're wrong," Jane told her. "It was a very brave decision. It's always better to get the things we dread over with, so we can move on."

"Amen," Ricky said. "Now I propose we all get out of this steam bath and go to lunch. A deli, perhaps?" He winked at Jane.

"Definitely," she said at once.

After casting one last, lingering look over her shoulder, Allie drew in a deep breath and led the way to the car, still clutching her bear. Ricky put the other items in the trunk, then drove them to a deli about a mile away.

Jane ordered her pastrami on rye and plucked a

pickle out of the jar on the table, even before he or Allie could take a good look at the menu.

When Allie ordered a cup of chicken soup, Jane stared at her in horror.

"That's not enough to keep a bird alive. Eat something that will put a little meat on your bones," she advised Allie. "You have to keep your strength up."

To Ricky's surprise, Allie deferred to her friend.

"What would you suggest?"

"Potato pancakes with apple sauce and sour cream," Jane said at once, then grinned. "I'll split it with you, and you can have half of my sandwich."

"Done," Allie agreed.

As they ate, Ricky watched with relief as the color came back into Allie's cheeks and her eyes lost that dull lifelessness. She was actually laughing again—albeit not very wholeheartedly—by the time they left.

At Jane's place she gave the older woman a fierce hug.

"I'll be over to see you this weekend," Jane promised. "We'll get started on those calls. You make a list of everyone you'd like me to contact. Till then you keep a stiff upper lip."

"I'll see to it," Ricky promised.

Jane gave him a hug, too. "I'm counting on it, young man. Our Allie needs you."

Ricky knew it was true, but in the back of his mind, he couldn't help wondering if the neediness was only temporary. And what would happen to the two of them when she was back on her feet again?

How crazy was it to dread the time when she would be ready to move away and begin her life over again? he asked himself.

When he got home from Pedro's excruciating concert later that night, he sat in the back yard as Allie slept and wondered how she had gotten under his skin so quickly. Today certainly told part of the story. He didn't think he'd ever met anyone more brave. He was in awe of her strength.

It was that strength that would take her away from him in the end, and he would have to let her go, because if ever there was a woman who needed to stand on her own two feet, it was Allie.

But maybe, in time, if he was very lucky, she would let him stand beside her.

## Chapter Ten

Allie sat on a chaise lounge in the back yard and cast surreptitious glances at Ricky, who was stretched out on the lounge chair next to hers. He was feigning sleep. She was sure of it. What she couldn't figure out was why. He'd been brooding and distant ever since they'd returned from their visit to what was left of her house the day before. She'd been relieved when he'd finally left to go to Pedro's concert.

Apparently, whatever was on his mind hadn't resolved itself by the time he returned, because he'd spent most of the night outside. She knew because she'd glanced out the window several times and seen him sitting right where he was now, a beer on the table beside him.

When she'd come downstairs first thing this morning, the bottle had been right where she'd seen it during the night and it was barely half-empty.

"You don't have to baby-sit me," she said eventually.

She saw his lips move slightly, but no word was formed. She interpreted that to be the equivalent of an acknowledging "Hmm?"

"I said I will be perfectly fine if you want to go out."

He opened his eyes then and glanced toward her. "Who said anything about going out?"

"You must be getting restless," she said.

"Not especially."

"Well, I certainly am."

He stood up so quickly she was sure he intended to seize the opportunity to take off.

"You're absolutely right," he said, and held out his hand. "Let's go."

"Go where?"

"Come on," he said, his eyes twinkling with a challenge. "Trust me."

Before she could second-guess herself, she jumped up. She told herself her eagerness was natural. She was sick of sitting around doing nothing. She'd finished every piece of paperwork Gina had brought by dinnertime the night before. Anything he had in mind would be an improvement. She ignored the little voice that taunted that this man could tempt her into doing things she would otherwise never consider. Her enthusiasm was all about being with him, not being active.

Before she could ask a single question, he'd grabbed her purse, a bottle of suntan lotion and their sunglasses.

"Are we going to the beach?" she asked, hurrying to keep up with him.

"You'll see."

En route to whatever their destination was, he pulled up to a small gourmet shop, ran inside and emerged with a cooler. "Lunch," he explained when she eyed it with curiosity.

Fifteen minutes later they pulled into a marina. Ricky led the way along a dock until he reached a small fishing boat. He stepped in and held out his hand.

"Yours, I hope," she said as she joined him.

"Tom's, but I have a key. There are fishing poles stashed onboard. Let me get this food into the refrigerator down in the galley, and we'll take off." His gaze narrowed. "You don't get seasick, do you?"

Allie grinned. "It's a little late to be asking, isn't it?"

"It would be too late if we were a mile offshore. Here there are still options."

"As far as I know, I don't get seasick."

"As far as you know," he repeated. "Does that mean you've never been out on a boat?"

"You've got it," she confirmed.

"Well, luckily, the water's like glass today. You should be fine. Do you swim?"

"In a pool," she said.

"I'll get you a life jacket while I'm down below," he said dryly.

Minutes later he started the boat's engine, cast off the lines and eased away from the dock. Allie stood at the railing and watched the marina disappear as they headed out into the bay. The breeze smelled of salt and maybe seaweed or mangroves. The kiss of the air against her bare skin counterpointed the sun's heat. Though the Miami skyline was never out of sight, it was as if they'd retreated into their own world. When they were a mile or so offshore, Ricky cut the engine. The boat bobbed gently on the water as he came to stand beside her.

"This is the first thing I do when I get back from a rescue operation overseas," he said.

She saw the ever-present worry lines in his face begin to ease. Without thinking, she reached up and touched his cheek. His skin was warm from the sun and rough with the beginning stubble of his beard. She'd never felt anything so masculine.

She wasn't sure of the precise moment when she became aware of the flare of heat in his eyes, but rather than withdraw her hand, she tentatively traced the outline of his mouth. A muscle in his jaw worked.

Then before she knew what he intended, he captured her hand where it was and drew one finger into his mouth in a slow, provocative move that made her heart leap in her chest. His gaze never left hers. Allie felt as if her entire world consisted of the blazing heat in his eyes and the sensation of his tongue against her finger.

"Do you have any idea what you do to me?" he murmured, releasing her hand with obvious reluctance.

Because she didn't think she could speak past the lump in her throat, she shook her head.

"I want to kiss you," he told her.

"Then do," she said, already feeling her breath hitch and her pulse begin to pound in anticipation. "Please."

His mouth claimed hers at once, almost as if he

feared she might change her mind. Hot, throbbing need ricocheted wildly through her. She tried to get closer, but he held her a careful distance away, allowing only their lips to touch with the kind of intimacy she craved.

"Why?" she murmured restlessly, desperately wanting something he seemed unwilling to offer.

She felt his lips move against hers and knew he was responding. She wanted to know the answer, but she needed the kisses more. Sweet, tender kisses. Urgent, demanding kisses. The pattern was unexpected, unpredictable and relentless. She had never known that kisses could be so shattering, so utterly magnificent in their own right. She was practically quivering with need by the time he stepped back and released her.

Blinking against the brilliance of the sunlight and the sudden abandonment, she stared at him. "Why?" she asked again.

He shoved his hands in his pockets and faced her with grim determination. "Because I didn't bring you out here to seduce you."

"Plans change," she said, forcing a light note into her voice.

A grin appeared and disappeared so quickly she almost missed it.

"Not this time," he said, his expression unyielding.

Still fighting the aftereffects of his kisses, she struggled for a cavalier attitude. "Mind telling me why?"

"I am not taking advantage of you, of the situation," he declared, seemingly to remind himself as well as to enlighten her.

She felt her temper stir. "That's very noble, but why do you get to make the call?"

"Because you're not thinking clearly."

"Oh?" She managed the word with deadly calm, but the pounding of her blood told another story.

"Don't look at me like that. You've been through a very traumatic time."

"But my brain still functions fairly well," she retorted. "I think I'm capable of making rational decisions."

"Rational ones, perhaps," he agreed. "But this isn't about rational. It's about hormones. The two are mutually exclusive."

The superior tone grated. "Okay, let me get this straight," she said, hanging on to her fury by a thread. "You—intelligent male creature that you are—can make a *rational* decision about seduction for both of us, but I—a mere female—cannot be counted on to do so for myself. Have I got that right?"

He scowled. "I don't see why you're getting so worked up. I'm trying to do the right thing here."

"What *you* consider to be the right thing," she corrected. "If that isn't the most ridiculous, most patronizing, *male* logic I have ever heard in my life, I don't know what is."

"Now, Allie…"

"Don't you 'Now, Allie' me!" she shouted. "I just might be inclined to do something irrationally female and knock you overboard."

He stared at her with obvious shock. "You wouldn't."

"Don't test me," she snapped.

She whirled around, stepped gingerly toward the

stairs leading belowdeck and retreated to the galley. She found herself a cold drink, popped the top and took a long, slow swallow, hoping to cool her parched throat and hot temper.

The man was a macho idiot. She'd been weak-kneed and willing, and he had rejected her. She didn't know which irritated her more—that he had been able to resist her, or that he'd actually thought she didn't know her own mind. Either way, it would be a cold day in hell before he got a second chance.

Women! Ricky sat on deck and wondered if he would ever understand the female of the species. He figured it was pretty doubtful, even for a man who'd grown up with four very perplexing sisters.

Frankly, up until the last week, his inability to grasp the complexities of the female mind hadn't mattered to him all that much, but for some idiotic reason he wanted to know what made Allie tick.

He was pretty sure he knew what ticked her off, though. What he viewed as honorable behavior apparently riled her no end. He had a hunch he could explain from now until they were both rocking in an old folks' home and she still wouldn't get it. He was beginning to wonder himself if he wasn't out of his mind. He'd had a woman who made him ache ready and willing to relieve that ache and he'd stopped her. Maybe he *did* need to have his head examined.

He would have given anything right now for something cold to drink, but it would take more than an insatiable thirst to make him wander belowdeck to cross paths with Allie. She was clearly in an unpredictable mood, and he was no saint. The next time she offered, he might not be nearly so concerned with what was right and honorable and decent.

He heard her footsteps coming up the stairs and forced himself to keep right on staring out to sea, his eyes shaded by very dark sunglasses. He almost jumped out of his seat when he felt the sprinkles of ice water on his chest.

"Damn, Allie," he muttered and looked up into eyes glinting with satisfaction.

"I thought you might want something to drink," she said sweetly.

"I'd rather have it in me than on me," he grumbled under his breath, but he accepted the can of soda, which was still dripping from being submerged in the cooler of ice. "Thank you."

"You're welcome," she said just as politely. "If you're hungry, I could bring up lunch."

He regarded her uncertainly. Was she trying to make amends for her overreaction? Or did she intend to find some way to spoil the food and poison him? Because he wasn't entirely sure, he said, "Not just yet." He wanted a little more time to get a fix on her mood.

He gestured toward the seat next to him. "Want to sit?"

"I'll stand."

"Whatever."

Unfortunately, her decision to stand put her legs at eye level. He couldn't seem to drag his gaze away from her bare, lightly tanned thighs. He wondered what she did to get that kind of muscle tone. He wondered how her skin would feel, how it would taste.

He wondered too blasted many things he had no business thinking about, he told himself sternly.

He looked up and saw that she was studying him with a frown.

"Everything okay?" she inquired.

"Perfect," he retorted irritably. "Everything is just perfect."

"Yes, it is, isn't it?" she murmured with a smug smile.

Then she turned and strolled to the bow of the boat, hips swaying. That sway was deliberate, Ricky concluded, as was that entire encounter. Apparently his sweet, vulnerable, brave Allie was dead set on revenge.

Ricky was pretty sure that the day, which had started with such promise, couldn't get any worse, but he was wrong. When he and Allie arrived at his house just after five—still barely speaking—he found the place crawling with people. Apparently his family had tired of waiting for an invitation to meet Allie and had decided to come calling.

If he was appalled by the timing, it was obvious that Allie was alarmed. When she spotted Maria and the boys, she clearly guessed the identity of the others. She cast a frantic look at him.

"Couldn't we run away?"

"We tried that once today and it didn't go so well," he pointed out. "It won't be so bad."

"Easy for you to say. It's your family."

"Which means I'll catch the brunt of the inquisition," he said. "They'll be nice to you."

He wasn't nearly as sure of that as he tried to appear. The gleam in his mother's eye as she approached the car was not reassuring. He'd seen that look before, directed at the men who were now his brothers-in-law.

His mother ignored him and headed straight for the door on Allie's side of the car.

"You must be Allie," she said, all but dragging Allie from the car and embracing her in a hug. "I am Enrique's mother. I've been so anxious to meet you, but my son kept telling me that I must wait until you have recovered. It is when you are *not* recovered that you need family around you, is it not? Men do not understand such things."

Allie cast a desperate look in his direction. "I suppose," she murmured, clearly not knowing what to make of this stranger who was already treating her like a member of the family.

"Come, meet the others," his mother commanded, not giving Allie much choice in the matter as she led her up the walk.

The two women disappeared inside the house, and Ricky breathed a sigh of relief. He exited the car slowly, grateful for his own reprieve. There was nothing he could do to save Allie, anyway. If he could just sneak around back, he might be able to hide out until the worst of the visit was over.

"Sorry, little brother," Maria said, joining him as he rounded the corner. "Inside. Allie needs you."

"Actually, she's not very happy with me at the moment."

"Oh? Why is that?"

"Long story and not one I'm inclined to discuss. Suffice it to say that the timing of your arrival sucks."

Maria laughed. "Maybe not. By the time Mama

extols all your virtues, Allie won't be able to resist you.''

Of course, her susceptibility to him wasn't exactly the issue, not the way his sister meant. Again, though, he refrained from explaining.

"Everyone's here?" he asked.

"Every single one of us, kids included," she said with a disgusting amount of glee. "Not to worry, though. Mama brought enough dinner for an army, with plenty for leftovers."

"You're all staying?"

"Well, of course. Mama's not about to cut short a chance to get to know a prospective daughter-in-law. She's been waiting for this day for too long."

Ricky wondered if it was too late to bolt. He could run faster than Maria, though her speed had improved somewhat since she'd started chasing after four active sons. He sighed and gave up on the idea. Allie would never forgive him if he abandoned her. He might not understand a lot about women, but he knew that much with absolute certainty.

He turned to his sister. "One hour," he declared firmly. "You get them all out of here in one hour. Allie needs her rest."

Maria chuckled. "Nice touch. All that concern is very sweet, but something tells me it's not Allie you're worried about. You want us gone before we start planning your wedding."

"Bite your tongue," he snapped, then stalked inside.

He found Allie sitting on the sofa between his mother and his father. His sisters were planted in the remaining chairs, while their husbands stood uneasily surveying the scene—probably recalling when they'd been in similar uncomfortable circumstances.

Nine children, all under the age of ten, were racing from room to room, enthusiastically chased by a barking Shadow, who rarely had an opportunity for such indoor antics. For once Ricky almost envied Allie her deafness. The noise level was earsplitting.

"Shadow, sit!" Ricky commanded. The dog flopped down at his feet at once, tail wagging. Unfortunately, the effect of the command did not extend to the children. He frowned at them and pointed toward the door. "Outside."

Maria's husband, Ben, winked at him. "I'll go with them. I know you want to stay right here in the center of things."

"Not especially," Ricky said, watching enviously as his brother-in-law made a hasty escape.

He turned his attention back to Allie. She looked a little dazed by the barrage of questions being flung at her.

"You must have been terrified during the storm," Elena said sympathetically. "Had you been here before during a hurricane?"

At the same time, Margarita was saying, "I understand you're a teacher. So am I. We'll have to have lunch one day and compare notes." She patted her huge belly. "I'll have plenty of time off once these babies get here."

"That's what you think," Daniela said. "You might not be at school, but you'll wish you were." She shuddered visibly. "Two babies at once. I can't imagine it."

"She will have me to help," his mother said.

His sisters exchanged a pained look.

"What?" his mother demanded indignantly. "An *abuela* will be in the way?"

Margarita lumbered to her feet and planted a kiss on her mother's cheek. "No, Mama, you will be a godsend. I couldn't manage without you."

"Then why do I get these looks from your sisters?" she demanded.

"Because they are ungrateful beasts," Margarita said. "They know I am your favorite."

His mother clucked her disapproval. "You know I do not have a favorite."

"Except Enrique!" they all chimed in a well-rehearsed chorus.

He frowned at the whole lot of them, his reaction as familiar as the ribbing.

The chatter continued fast and furiously. It was peppered with Spanish. Allie sat amid the hubbub, blinking rapidly and trying to keep up, but Ricky could see from the way her head bobbed from person to person that it was a lost cause. Too many people were talking at once, much of it in a language she didn't understand.

Oddly, though, she didn't seem to be as frustrated as he would have expected. In fact, her lips had curved into a half smile and her eyes sparkled with delight. When she caught sight of him, the smile faded.

"Uh-oh," Maria murmured behind him. "You really are in trouble, aren't you?"

"I told you I was."

"Why don't I rescue Allie and take her into the kitchen? She looks as if she could use a breather from all the commotion. She and I can put out the food, while you fend off the inquiring minds.

Mama's got that look in her eye, the one she reserves for unsuspecting potential mates. My Ben still shudders when he sees it. Says he'd never been so terrified in his life. Allie is definitely no match for that look and the questions that come with it.''

"Fantastic idea," Ricky said gratefully. "In fact, why don't you take her right on out the back door and go to some nice quiet restaurant for dinner? You can bring her back after everyone's gone home."

"And have Mama on my case for a month? I don't think so."

Maria crossed the room and bent down to speak to Allie. She nodded at once and stood up to follow the older woman. When their mother started to rise, Maria shot her a warning look that kept her in place.

After Allie and Maria had gone, the attention that had been riveted on Allie turned to Ricky.

"I've got nothing to say on the subject," he announced before they could start in. He looked straight at his father. "How about those Dolphins? Think they've got any shot at the Super Bowl this year?"

"Football," his mother said derisively. "If you think we came over here to discuss football, you are *loco*."

He planted a smacking kiss on her cheek. "I know it's not what you came to discuss, but Allie is off-limits. You'll scare her out of her wits."

"She was not frightened by us," his mother said.

"Overwhelmed, then. Do you realize that with all of you talking at once, she couldn't possibly know what you were saying? She can only read one set of lips at a time. Didn't you wonder why she never answered a single question?"

His mother's expression faltered. "Oh, I am so sorry. I never even considered." She leaped to her feet. "I must apologize."

"Leave it alone for now," Ricky advised. "Give her some time with Maria."

His mother looked torn. She clearly hated the thought that she might have inadvertently offended Allie, when her intentions had been only to welcome her into the family.

"Do as he says," his father advised, tugging on his wife's hand until she relented and sat back down.

"Thanks," Ricky said, a little surprised to have his father's backing. Usually his father went along with whatever his beloved wife wanted.

"So," his mother said, her expression determined in light of their objections. "How about those Dolphins?"

Her daughters erupted into laughter. "Mama, do you even know who the Dolphins are?" Elena asked.

"Of course I do," his mother said indignantly. "But why anyone would choose to watch American football, rather than soccer is beyond me."

It was an old argument and one his family settled into readily. Satisfied that they were temporarily distracted, Ricky wandered into the kitchen just in time to hear Allie ask plaintively, "Do you think there's something wrong with me, besides my hearing, I mean?"

Maria caught a glimpse of him hesitating in the doorway and scowled before reassuring Allie, "There is nothing wrong with you. My brother is a dolt."

Ricky concluded that he was out of favor in the kitchen. He had two choices, he could go in there and defend himself for the second time that day, or he could go back to the living room and risk having the conversation shift from football back to his marital intentions. He opted for the kitchen, dangerous though it was.

"Need any help?" he inquired as he joined his sister and Allie.

"Everything's under control," Maria said. "I'll just start putting things on the table in the dining room. We'll do this buffet-style, since your table's not big enough for all of us to sit around it. The kids can eat outside."

She deliberately turned her back on Allie before adding, "Use this time alone with Allie to bail yourself out of trouble, baby brother. I don't know what you did, but it's obvious you hurt her."

"I don't think it's something that can be fixed in a few minutes," he said.

"Try," she ordered, letting the kitchen door swing shut behind her. "She's the best thing that ever happened to you. Don't blow it."

When they were alone, Allie regarded him nervously. "I like your family," she said.

"I'm sorry if they bombarded you with too many personal questions. It's a nosy crowd."

"I didn't mind." She grinned. "They didn't wait for answers, anyway. To tell you the truth, I had trouble keeping up with what they were saying."

"They didn't realize—" he began, but she cut him off.

"I'm used to that. You don't have to apologize. It's better sometimes when people forget I'm deaf. For a few minutes, even though I'm left out of the conversation, I feel almost normal."

"Allie, you *are* normal," he said fiercely, recalling the plaintive question she'd just asked Maria. "Just because you can't hear doesn't mean there's anything wrong with you."

She stared at him, clearly surprised by his vehemence. "You really mean that, don't you?"

"Well, of course I do," he said emphatically. "You're an amazing woman. Most of the time I completely forget that you can't hear. I have to remind myself that in certain circumstances you are at a disadvantage."

To his dismay, tears welled up and spilled down her cheeks. He knelt in front of her and brushed them from her cheeks. "What is it? What did I say?"

She clasped his hand and pressed a kiss to his palm. "You said everything just right," she whispered. "Most people, men especially, are too solicitous. They never forget that I have a disability and, because of that, they never let me forget it, either. There's no ignoring the fact that I can't hear, but once in a while it is so amazing to be able to pretend that it doesn't matter."

"It doesn't matter, not to me," he said. "My only regret is that you are missing some of the things you used to love, like your music. I can't even imagine how difficult that must have been for you to accept. It's no wonder you were so angry that I just walked away from my art."

"Yes, because you could do it and you don't."

"It's not in my soul, the way music was in yours. It's something I enjoy, something I'm good at, but it's not my passion."

"Sometimes I can still hear the music in my head," she told him, her expression filled with sorrow. She reached out and touched a finger to his lips. ''Do you know what I really regret?''

He shook his head.

''That I've never heard the sound of your voice.''

Ricky felt the sting of his own tears burning at the back of his eyes. ''Oh, *querida,* you hear everything that's important.''

Maybe one day he would even risk letting her hear what was in his heart.

*Chapter Eleven*

Allie declined an invitation from Ricky's mother to join the family for Sunday dinner. Her emotions were still ragged from the afternoon on the boat, the surprise visit of his family and from the things he'd said to her in the kitchen. She had the uneasy feeling that she was tumbling head over heels in love with a man she barely knew. Until she understood their relationship more fully, she didn't dare risk falling for his family, too.

"I don't understand," Jane said, when Allie tried to explain it to her. "You're crazy about him. He's crazy about you. Where's the problem?"

"It's too soon," she said stubbornly. "How can I trust what I'm feeling? Ricky certainly doesn't. He flat-out told me that I can't possibly know my own mind."

Jane chuckled. "How did you react when he suggested that?"

"I was furious."

"I can imagine."

Allie regarded her plaintively. "But what if he's right? What if the circumstances are just so volatile that I would have fallen for any man who plucked me out of that rubble? It's possible."

"Did you fall for Tom?"

She frowned at the absurdity of the question. "No, of course not."

"He was there, too," Jane said.

"But he wasn't the one who was talking me through it. He wasn't the one who actually brought me out."

"But if he had been, you would have fallen for him instead?" Jane asked, her skepticism plain.

Allie tried to envision herself falling for the sweet, gentle giant who was Ricky's partner. She'd spent a little time with him since the storm and hadn't felt so much as a tingle of attraction, though he was more classically handsome than Ricky.

"No," she admitted slowly. "He's a very nice man, but he doesn't do anything at all for me."

"Now we're getting somewhere." Jane regarded her with a sly expression. "Are you the first woman Ricky has ever saved?"

"No," Allie conceded.

"As far as you know, has he ever invited any of the others to live with him?"

"I'm not living with him," she argued. "I'm just staying here temporarily."

Jane rolled her eyes. "Whatever. Has he done this sort of thing before?"

"I don't think so."

"Then why do you suppose he picked you?"

Allie frowned. "If I knew that, this would be a whole lot less complicated."

"Sometimes love is only as complicated as we choose to make it."

"Whatever that means."

"It means, my darling girl, that love itself is simple. Resisting it is what makes it tricky. You're busy finding excuses for not being in love, instead of seizing it as the wonderful gift it is."

"Don't two people have to seize it at the same time?"

Jane grinned at the plaintive question. "That does help," she agreed. "Maybe I'll explain the concept to Ricky when he drives me home later this afternoon."

"Don't you dare. I don't want him to think we've spent the whole day sitting around talking about him."

"But that is exactly what we have done," Jane said.

"Then it's time to change the subject. How are things with you and your sister?" she asked, knowing it was a question that was guaranteed to send Jane off on another tangent. "They can't be too bad, because you look fabulous. You've even got a new haircut. Very flattering. You look ten years younger. You let the hairdresser put a blond rinse on it, too, didn't you?"

"I know what you're doing," Jane responded pointedly, even though she looked pleased by the compliment. "But I'm not going to forget about this business with Ricky."

"Then I suppose I'll just have to come along when he takes you home so I can protect my own interests."

"Suit yourself," Jane said easily. "As for my sister, the woman is flat-out crazy. Do you know what she's done now?"

Allie settled back for the tirade, relieved not to have to defend her feelings for Ricky for the moment. Maybe things would be better after tomorrow. She intended to go back to work. They wouldn't be spending nearly as much time together. And soon she would move out.

That would be the real test, she concluded. If something were meant to happen between her and Ricky, then her moving to her own place wouldn't be the end of things. She resolved to start looking for a short-term rental the minute she finished up her first day back at the clinic on Monday.

Unfortunately, events conspired against her.

Her last patient was four-year-old Kimi Foley and she could see why Gina had expressed concern about the little girl. She wasn't keeping up with her sign language lessons nearly as well as Allie had hoped she would.

"Are you mad at me?" the child signed at the end of the session, her expression worried.

"Never," Allie reassured her, giving her a hug.

"But I keep forgetting."

"That's okay. You just need a little more practice at home."

Kimi's sweet little face fell. "How? Nobody at home will learn."

Allie bit back a curse. Jessica Foley was a good

mother, but she was overwhelmed by the responsibility of four other children besides Kimi. Coping with Kimi's hearing loss was more of a burden than she'd been able to manage so far. Getting her daughter to the clinic for the twice-a-week sessions was about all she'd been willing to do. Staying for her own classes had been out of the question. She had flatly refused.

"I'll pick it up from Kimi," she had assured Allie, but the futility of that promise was increasingly evident.

As for Derrick Foley, he worked two jobs to try to provide for his family. He'd picked Kimi up on a few occasions and, though the love he had for his little girl was obvious, he still seemed to be in a state of denial that her disability was permanent and required any sort of adjustments on his part to help her deal with it. When he spoke to her, he raised his voice as if somehow that would help her to hear him.

The Foleys weren't the first family Allie had seen struggle to adapt to the needs of a hearing-impaired child, but it never failed to sadden her. As in her own case and Kimi's, it seemed to be worse when the hearing loss was sudden and unexpected.

"You and I will work harder," she told Kimi. "And I'll speak to your mom again about lessons. If she can't do it, what about your older sister. She's ten, right?"

The child's expression brightened at the suggestion. "Marty would do it. I know she would."

"Then I'll see if I can arrange it," Allie promised.

"I love you," Kimi signed.

"I love you, too," Allie told her. "Now let's go outside and see if your mom's here."

Mrs. Foley was sitting in her car, waiting at the curb. Allie walked Kimi to the car, but when she tried to speak to her mother, Mrs. Foley waved her off with the announcement that she was running late. She pulled away from the curb before Allie could say a word.

Allie sighed heavily and dragged back inside. Apparently, she wasn't nearly as recovered as she'd thought she was. She was exhausted, but she was determined to stick around for the weekly staff meeting.

Gina took one look at her and vetoed her plan. "You're pale. You need to go home."

"I'm back full-time," Allie insisted to her boss. "Give me five minutes to grab a cup of coffee, and I'll join you in the conference room."

She had assumed that Gina accepted her word as final, but apparently she was wrong. The meeting had barely started when it was interrupted by Ricky's arrival. Gina beamed at him.

"You made good time," she said.

"You called him?" Allie asked, stunned by the betrayal.

"We had a deal," Gina said. "I was to call if you resisted my common sense advice. Now go home. Get some rest. We'll see you in the morning."

Sorely tempted to plant herself right where she was and refuse to budge, she changed her mind when she met Ricky's determined gaze. She could always quit just to express her displeasure, but she managed to leave the room without taking such a drastic step. She loved her job. And tomorrow she would tell Gina that she was perfectly capable of deciding whether she felt well enough to spend an hour at a stupid staff meeting.

Since that discussion had to wait, she settled for snapping at Ricky. "Why aren't you back at work?"

"I was. And I'll be there again as soon as I get you home. I have my beeper on, in case they need me in the meantime."

"I don't appreciate you barging in here like this," she said as she gathered up the work she intended to do at home that night.

"I didn't barge in," he said patiently. "Your boss called me."

"She had no business doing that."

"She cares about you."

"That's very sweet, I'm sure, but I can look after myself."

"Then do it. Go home and take a nap."

"I'm not tired," she said, perfectly aware that she sounded like a sullen child resisting bedtime.

"So you say," he retorted mildly.

Naturally, she had to go and prove him right. Five minutes in the car and she couldn't keep her eyes open. She wasn't even aware of arriving at the house. She woke up as he shifted her into his arms to carry her inside.

"What are you doing?" she demanded, struggling to get down.

It was a wasted effort. He merely chuckled and held on tighter, clearly unimpressed by her grouchiness. "Three guesses what I'm doing."

She pushed against the solid wall of his chest. "Put me down."

His gaze locked with hers. "Give me a break, Allie. Two minutes in my arms, maybe three. Is that so much to ask?''

Incredulity replaced indignation. "What are you saying, that you're enjoying this?''

He settled her a little more tightly against his chest. "What do you think?''

If she were forced to be totally honest, it wasn't so bad from her perspective, either. She sighed and relented, then looped an arm around his neck. "Go for it, Wilder. Enjoy yourself.''

She had to admit that snuggling against him wasn't exactly a sacrifice. The only problem would be that when they got to her bed, he was going to unceremoniously dump her there and leave her all alone.

She pressed her face against his neck. But for two minutes, maybe three, she could pretend that he might not.

Ricky was pretty sure Allie Matthews was going to drive him out of his mind. Now that they were both back at work, they were uneasily struggling to fit into each other's routines. He'd actually believed that once they were both out of the house, life would be less complicated. He'd anticipated giving her a wide berth so he could keep his hormones in check, but it wasn't turning out quite that way.

She was on his mind night and day. He told himself it was because he hadn't slept with her. If they'd gotten that out of the way, he wouldn't feel this constant aching need. He would be halfway to being over her.

Instead, he was sex deprived and sleep deprived. With every moment that passed, he felt himself more and more drawn to Allie's amazing serenity, her strength and determination to recover fully and to reclaim her shattered life. Of course, her tendency to want to rush it annoyed him. She was going to have a relapse if she kept it up.

Monday had been a perfect example. When he'd gone to pick her up at school, it was plain that she was dead on her feet, but she'd still been furious because he and Gina had conspired to make her go home. If the woman didn't have sense enough to know when to call it quits, how was he supposed to believe she had sense enough to know her own mind when it came to him? Fortunately, he'd been smart enough not to ask her that. The memory of the last time he'd made that suggestion still burned in his head.

He sighed heavily, glanced up and suddenly realized he was surrounded by half a dozen grinning firefighters.

"What?" he demanded.

"Definitely a woman," one of them said with a knowing expression on his face.

"Has to be," another agreed.

"The beautiful Allie," Tom informed them. "She has our Enrique dancing at the end of a string."

He frowned at the teasing. "I am not..."

"Were you or were you not completely unaware that we have been standing here for the past ten minutes?" Tom asked.

"Yes, but—"

"Were you or were you not occupied with thoughts of your lovely houseguest?"

"I don't have to answer that."

Tom took a mocking bow as the others hooted. "I rest my case."

"You want to talk about women?" Ricky inquired lazily. "Shall we discuss the ex-wife who is never far from your thoughts? Shall we mention the fact that you have been dropping by her house, interviewing her damn dates?"

"I have not," Tom began, his face flushed with indignation. "Okay, I have been over there a few times."

"I rest *my* case," Ricky said.

"We're both a couple of saps," Tom concluded sorrowfully.

"Speak for yourself," Ricky retorted. "You've been there, done that. You ought to know better. I'm still feeling my way here."

"An interesting turn of phrase," one of his co-workers declared. "What do you suppose he means by that, men?"

"Oh, go to blazes," Ricky muttered.

"Not a suggestion to be made lightly in a fire station," Tom pointed out, then sighed. "But I understand the sentiment."

"What am I supposed to do?" Ricky asked.

"Like I would know," Tom responded woefully.

"Then leave me alone to think," Ricky pleaded. "I have to figure this out."

What was it about Allie? She was nothing like the women who usually attracted him. He was used to glib chatter and easy flirting. Allie got charmingly rattled at his teasing.

Moreover, he found that she expected—no, demanded—more, in her quiet, intense way. It was the way she looked at him, disappointment in her eyes, when he evaded a question or offered a less-than-truthful response. She always seemed to know, too, which was as disconcerting as it was flattering.

Then there was his family. They had taken to Allie as if she were one of their own. Each one of his sisters had called to express approval. His mother had taken him aside on Sunday to ask a million and one questions about his relationship with the woman living in his house. Even his father had commented at dinner that he considered Allie to be a keeper.

"The woman's got a good, level head on her shoulders," his father had told him. "You could do worse."

Even the kids had chimed in, his nephews declaring Allie to be "a real babe."

He frowned at each of the boys in turn. "What do you know about babes?"

"Hey, we're guys, too," Ray had declared, skinny little chest puffed out.

"And Mama says if we're not careful, we're gonna turn out to be flirts like you," Maria's oldest chimed in. "She says it as if it's a bad thing."

Ricky had glanced across the table at his sister. "A bad thing?"

"If all you do is flirt and never take any woman seriously, you'll wind up all alone in your old age," she said.

"Don't you think it's a little soon to be worrying about my old age?" he inquired.

"You're thirty, baby brother," Elena pointed out.

"By now you should have two or three children," his mother declared. "It's your responsibility to see that your father's name is carried on."

"Don't put pressure on him," his father said, in a

rare contradiction of his wife. "Marriage is a big step. He shouldn't take it before he's ready."

"Somebody has to push him," Maria said. "Otherwise he'll still be dating when he's in the old folks' home."

"You're just jealous because I've been with more than one woman and you've spent your entire life with one man," Ricky had taunted.

His sister's cheeks had flushed, and she'd reached for her husband's hand. "When you find the best right off, there's no need to waste time sifting through second bests. Which reminds me, baby brother, you owe us a weekend of baby-sitting."

Ricky envied the love glowing in her eyes as she and Benny exchanged a long look. "I'll check my calendar, and we'll work it out," he promised. "Try to keep your hands off each other until then. There are children in the room."

"You're just jealous, *niño*."

"Okay, enough," his father declared. "Leave the man alone. He will do whatever he's going to do without our interference."

"Thank you, Papa," Ricky said.

"Don't thank me. I'm one of those who think you're a fool if you let Allie get away. I'm just not going to waste my breath trying to convince you."

As Ricky recalled the exchange, he felt the same pressure building up inside him. His family had too many expectations. By contrast, it appeared Allie had none. She hadn't asked for anything except a little honesty, a little less interference. Worse, he had a hunch she was gearing up to move out, and he had no idea how to stop her.

When his shift finally ended, he debated accepting

Tom's invitation to stop off for a few beers but finally declined.

"Going home?" Tom asked. "Do you and Allie have plans?"

"No, no plans." Now that she was getting a ride home with one of her friends, he couldn't even be sure she would be there, but he wanted to head over there in case she was.

"What about later?" Tom asked. "Want to get together? Maybe go on a double date?"

Ricky regarded him with curiosity. "You have a date?"

"With Nikki," he confessed.

"That's a surprise. How'd you convince your ex to go on a date?"

"Actually, I told her you and Allie would be along to chaperone. She's anxious to meet the woman who has you tied in knots."

"What happens if we don't show up?"

"My goose is cooked. She'll probably refuse to leave the house," he said, looking totally dejected.

Ricky took pity on him. "Okay, I'll see what I can do. I'll call you at Nikki's in an hour."

Tom's expression brightened. "Thanks. I owe you."

"Yes. You do."

When he got home, he found Allie in the kitchen staring at the contents of the refrigerator. She was barefoot and dressed in shorts and a tank top. She'd scooped her hair into a careless ponytail. She looked as if she was barely out of her teens and sexy as sin, all at the same time. He had to resist the urge to sneak up behind her and press a kiss to her bare nape.

"I know you're there," she said, startling him. She turned slowly, her expression serious.

"How did you know that?"

A grin tugged at her lips. "It's probably best that I keep that little secret to myself. It comes in handy."

He decided that was worth further thought at another time. "You can close the refrigerator door," he said. "We're going out for dinner."

He wasn't sure what reaction he'd expected to his announcement. Even as he uttered the words, he realized he should have phrased it as a question. To his surprise she seemed relieved.

"Good thing. The cupboard is bare. Where are we going?"

For some reason her unexpected agreeability annoyed him. "That's it? Just okay and where are we going?"

She gave him a perplexed look. "Did you want an argument?"

"Not really, but I usually get one."

"You mean because you're usually issuing edicts, rather than inquiring about my preferences?"

He winced at the direct hit. "Pretty much."

She laughed. "Every once in a while your arrogance coincides with my own desires. Why waste time arguing when that happens? I don't fight with you just for the thrill of it."

"Funny. I was beginning to think that was how you got your kicks," he murmured, forgetting for a moment that just keeping his voice low wouldn't prevent her from knowing what he'd said.

To emphasize his mistake, she tapped his lips. "I saw that."

Her touch, as light and teasing as it was, set off

all the pent-up hunger he'd been fighting for days. He reached for her and dragged her to him, his mouth closing over hers just as she uttered a little gasp of surprise.

He was only dimly aware that she wasn't struggling, wasn't even attempting to protest. He was too lost in the taste of her, in the way her body molded itself to his, the way one foot trailed up his calf as she fitted herself more snugly against his instant arousal.

Sweet heaven, the woman was a witch. Cool and calm one minute, she drove him to a frenzy as he tried to get a reaction. The next minute she was all heat and heart-stopping temptation. How was a man supposed to cope with a woman who could change moods on a dime? A woman who could look like an angel and kiss like a sinner?

Right this second Ricky would have given everything he owned to be able to scoop her up and carry her off to his bed and take full advantage of everything she was offering. He doubted even his iron will and sense of honor could have prevented it. Only the very dim memory of his commitment to his best friend nagged at him, until he finally released Allie with a shuddering sigh of regret.

"One of these days we're going to finish this," he said on a ragged breath.

"Now seems like as good a time as any," she said, her expression dazed and hopeful.

"Tom's waiting for us."

She stared at him blankly. "Tom? What does he have to do with this?"

"He finally managed to convince his ex-wife to go out on a date."

"And that matters to you and me because...?"

"She'll only go if we go."

Allie regarded him with fascination. "Why is that?"

"She wants to meet you more than she wants to steer clear of Tom."

"Okay, back up. They're divorced, correct?"

Ricky nodded.

"Then why do they want to go out at all?"

"According to my mother, they're still in love."

"What do you think?"

"No question in my mind that he's still in love with her. I haven't spoken to Nikki, but my mother assures me that the feeling is mutual."

"Then why on earth did they get a divorce in the first place?"

"Because they're both too bullheaded to compromise. She wants him to quit his job and go to work in her father's business. He loves what he does as much as I do. We're both danger junkies."

All of the color seemed to drain out of Allie's face. She quickly turned away and started for the door, but not before he'd seen that something was terribly wrong.

"I'll get ready," she said, her voice a little too quiet, a little too subdued.

Ricky snagged her wrist. "Hey, what just happened?"

"Nothing," she said stiffly.

"Allie, talk to me. One minute you were full of questions about Tom and Nikki, the next you looked as if I'd kicked the stuffing out of that favorite teddy bear of yours."

She shook her head. "It doesn't matter. We'd better hurry if we're going to meet your friends."

This time when she pulled away, Ricky let her go. But he had a feeling it would be a long time before he could shake the questions stirred by her odd behavior. He had a hunch the answers were even more important than he could imagine.

## Chapter Twelve

Allie wasn't sure why it hadn't sunk in sooner that what had been a rare and terrifying experience for her was something that Ricky did all the time. By his own admission, he thrived on taking risks. He hadn't built a career around saving lives because it was simply something that needed to be done or even as a way to prove to his father that he was macho as well as artistic. He did it because he loved the danger inherent in exploring collapsed buildings for survivors.

She had been caught by surprise, trapped in the rubble of her own home, alone and terrified for hours. He had considered rescuing her to be little more than a game, pitting his skill against Mother Nature's precarious aftermath.

Of course he was a well-trained expert. Of course he understood the risks and no doubt did everything in his power to minimize them. But the bottom line was he was the kind of man who would be easily bored by anything less than the extraordinary challenge of a dangerous profession.

How could he possibly be attracted to anything less in a woman? No wonder he'd never settled down with one woman. He needed the variety to avert boredom. As for her, she must seem incredibly dull, just an ordinary teacher, who couldn't even share in some of the activities most people took for granted, like music and dancing.

She realized glumly that these were definitely issues she was going to have to wrestle with, preferably sooner rather than later, and preferably without Ricky nagging at her for answers. She had hoped to get out of the kitchen without revealing her dismay, but obviously he'd noticed her reaction, even if he hadn't understood the reason for it. He wouldn't be satisfied with her evasion for long.

Thankful that they wouldn't be spending the evening alone, she rushed to get ready. She even managed to forget her own dilemma when they joined Tom and his ex-wife.

Allie liked Nikki at once. She had a warm smile and an exuberant personality. From the minute Allie walked through Nikki's front door, the other woman treated her as if they were old friends with a million things to catch up on.

"We have to talk," she told Allie, drawing her into the comfortably furnished living room of a Spanish-style home on a narrow waterway in Coral Gables. She gestured dismissively toward the men. "Let them fend for themselves. Tom knows his way around."

Tom looked disappointed, but he dutifully led Ricky off toward another part of the house.

Amused, Allie watched them leave. "I don't think this is what Tom had in mind," she suggested innocently.

"I'm sure it's not," Nikki agreed cheerfully. "I stopped doing what Tom expected on the day I divorced him. Actually before that. He didn't think I'd file to end the marriage in the first place. The man has a monumental ego. It serves him well in his work, but in his personal life..." She shrugged. "He needs to get over it."

It was an amazing display of bravado, but Allie didn't buy it. "You didn't think Tom would let you go through with the divorce, did you?"

Nikki stared at her in surprise. "How did you figure that out? No one else did. Well, except for Ricky's mother. She saw straight through me."

"And once you'd started the whole divorce thing, you didn't know how to stop it?"

The other woman sighed. "Pretty stupid, huh?"

"Not stupid. It was a drastic measure and it didn't work. I imagine you had your reasons for trying it."

"Oh, yes," Nikki said fervently. "That job of his scares me to death."

The response hit a little too close to what Allie had been thinking earlier. "But you knew what he did when you met, correct?"

"I thought he would be ready to stop once we started talking about having a family. I offered him an alternative, working for my father. I didn't care whether he did that or something else. I just wanted him to be safe. Instead of even trying to see my point, he accused me of trying to change him. He told me he wasn't cut out for a desk job and he never would be.''

"And you couldn't live with that," Allie surmised.

Nikki shrugged. "I didn't think I could, but now that I've been through the alternative—living without him—I know it's worse. I still worry myself sick every single time he's raced off to some disaster. I still sit by the phone, then panic when it rings. Thankfully, so far it's been Tom checking in to let me know he's okay."

"He calls even though you're divorced?"

"Every night he's gone," she said.

"Have you told him what you've figured out? That the divorce didn't give you the peace of mind you'd expected it to?"

Nikki sighed. "No."

"Why not?"

"Too much pride, I suppose. I keep hoping that being without me will be just as hard on him. I'm pretty sure it is, too, but I haven't seen any evidence that he's willing to consider a compromise."

"And do what instead?" What would be the compromise between a desk job and slip-sliding into a mountain of debris that could kill a man with one false step?

"I wish I knew." She gave Allie a penetrating look. "What about you? Are you okay with what Ricky does?"

"To be honest, I don't think it sank in until tonight what he does. He said something that caught me off guard. It shouldn't have, but it did."

Nikki looked surprised by the response. "How can that be? You met when he rescued you."

"I know. I guess I was so wrapped up in the relief of being saved that I forgot all about the risks he took to get me out of there. And somehow I completely missed the fact that he does that kind of thing all the time, that it wasn't some sort of heroic fluke."

"Now that you've realized it, are you going to stick it out or bail?"

Allie's gaze strayed toward the direction in which the men had gone. "I wish I knew," she admitted candidly, then shrugged. "Of course, it's not exactly an issue. Ricky and I are just friends."

Nikki stared at her, then burst out laughing. "Oh, my," she said eventually. "Listen to the two of us. We're both delusional. I think my ex-husband is going to suddenly convert to some nine-to-five life and you think there's nothing going on between you and Ricky."

"There isn't," Allie insisted.

Nikki patted her hand. "Tell yourself that all you want. I saw the way he looked at you."

"How?"

A grin spread across Nikki's face. "The same way you looked at him, like a lovesick teenager."

Well, hell.

The evening wasn't going at all the way Ricky had anticipated. Even after they reached the club where they'd gone for drinks after dinner, Allie and Nikki had had their heads together every second, giggling like a couple of schoolgirls over jokes they apparently saw no need to share. Tom didn't seem to mind, but it was driving Ricky crazy. What the heck did they have to talk about? They'd just met.

He finally decided enough was enough. He stood

up and put his hand under Allie's elbow. When she turned a startled look in his direction, he said, "Dance?"

"But I don't—"

"You can," he retorted, exerting a little pressure to encourage her to get to her feet. He glanced pointedly toward Tom and then Nikki. "I'm sure they'd like to dance, too."

Allie nodded at once. "Of course." She beamed at Nikki, who was regarding her ex-husband warily.

Before Allie could comment, Ricky urged her toward the dance floor. The music was slow, which was why he'd chosen that moment to insist on the dance. He could pull Allie close and demonstrate the rhythm of the song with the movements of his body.

For an instant she tensed against him, but then he felt her slowly relax.

"What's the song?" she asked, her gaze on his.

He told her the title of the old love song, and her expression brightened. He could hear her starting to hum the melody from memory. She found the rhythm on her own, without his guidance, then returned his gaze, her expression pleased.

"Told you so," he said.

"Told me what?"

"That you could dance."

"Because I remember the song," she said, then added wistfully, "I used to be able to play it on the violin."

"Have you played at all since you lost your hearing?"

She looked shocked by the question. "Of course not."

"Why not? You can still read music, can't you?"

"Yes, but—" Her expression faltered. Tears welled up. "I just can't. It would be too frustrating not to be able to hear it, not to know if I made a mistake."

He saw how much the loss of playing hurt her. "Some people would consider that an advantage," he said. "You could play in blissful ignorance. I'm sure Pedro would be happy to loan you his violin, and Maria would consider it a blessing if you'd keep it."

"No," she said fiercely. "Never."

He touched her cheek, tried to smooth away the lines of tension that had formed around her mouth. "I'm sorry. I was just hoping it might give you back something you'd lost."

"No. It would just make it a thousand times worse." She buried her face against his shoulder.

He wasn't quite ready to let the idea rest. He held her away from him and looked into her eyes. "Until tonight, you thought you'd never be able to dance again, but look at you now. It's something to think about."

To emphasize the point, he gathered her close and spun her around the dance floor in a series of intricate steps that she followed without a single stumble. The color rose in her cheeks and the sparks returned to her eyes. By the time the music stopped, she was laughing.

"Okay, okay, I can dance, but only if I hang on to you for dear life."

"And the problem with that is?" he asked, his gaze locked with hers.

Her bright-eyed expression faltered. "You won't

always be here,'' she whispered so low that he could barely hear her over the music.

Ricky wanted to deny it, wanted to tell her that she would always be able to turn to him, but the commitment terrified him. The only thing that terrified him more was the prospect of losing her.

Yet over the next few days that was exactly what he sensed was happening. Allie was still sharing the house, but there was a growing distance between them, a distance he didn't understand and couldn't seem to bridge.

Her strength was back and she seemed to be settling into a comfortable routine that didn't include him. She spent her days at work and her evenings with friends or locked up in her room doing paperwork for the clinic. He'd spotted her studying the classified ads for apartments on more than one occasion—though, thankfully, the rental market was tighter than ever because of the number of families displaced by the hurricane.

He was pretty sure he'd go nuts if he couldn't think of some way to shake that scary composure, that carefully polite facade that greeted him over the breakfast table.

He debated confronting her, asking why she'd suddenly withdrawn. He'd traced it back to the evening they'd spent with Nikki and Tom, but Tom was absolutely no help when Ricky questioned him about whether he'd noticed any reason why Allie might be ticked off.

''She seemed okay to me,'' Tom told him.

''And Nikki hasn't said anything?''

''Believe it or not, on those rare occasions when

I actually spend time with my ex-wife, you are not the topic of conversation,'' Tom said.

Ricky heard the edginess in his friend's voice. "How is that going, by the way? Are you making any progress?"

"It depends on what you call progress," Tom said. "Her string of admirers seems to be dwindling, but she still gets all huffy when I suggest we go out. I'm running out of ideas and patience."

"Tell me about it," Ricky said grimly. He made up his mind that he had to do something to break this unspoken standoff between him and Allie.

He had a hunch based on past experience that a kiss would do it. He just had to find the excuse—or the right occasion—for stealing one.

Although his schedule at work could be unpredictable, it appeared he had the weekend off. He concluded that Saturday would be the perfect opportunity for the two of them to spend some quality time together. He broached the subject over breakfast on Friday.

Reaching across the table, he tapped Allie's hand to distract her from the morning paper. "Do you have plans for tomorrow?" he asked when her startled gaze met his.

For an instant he actually thought he saw panic flare in her eyes, but she finally shook her head. "No. Why?"

"I thought we might spend the day together."

"You don't have to do that. I'm fine on my own now. I'm sure there are plenty of things you'd rather be doing than baby-sitting a houseguest who's probably overstayed her welcome."

The last part of her response snagged his attention.

"You have not overstayed your welcome. Have I said anything at all to make you think that? If I have, I'm sorry. You're welcome to stay here as long as you want to. In fact, I insist on it."

She avoided his gaze. "You don't have to be polite. I know this was supposed to be temporary. In fact, I was thinking of spending Saturday looking at a couple of apartments."

Ricky felt his gut clench at the confirmation that she was itching to move out. The very thought of it made him crazy. "Don't be ridiculous," he snapped. "Why should you spend money on an apartment when I have room here?"

"I must be cramping your style."

"Allie, where is this coming from?" he asked, barely curbing his impatience. "I thought we were doing okay here."

She regarded him guiltily. "I'm sorry. You've been wonderful. I just feel as if I'm imposing on you. I need to get back on my own."

"On your own? Or away from me? Why?"

She stood up, her movements hurried. "I have to get to work. Can we talk about this another time?"

She rushed out of the room, not waiting for a response. Rick stared after her.

"Well, what the hell was that all about?" he murmured when she'd gone.

He grabbed the phone and punched out Nikki's number. "I need to talk to you," he said when she answered.

"Okay, talk, but if this is about Tom you're wasting your breath."

"It's not about Tom, though I could give you an

earful on the subject. Another time, though. Do you have any idea what's up with Allie?''

''Allie? Is she okay?'' she asked at once, sounding genuinely concerned.

''That's what I'm asking you. Ever since that night the four of us went out, she's been acting all weird. Do you know what that's about?''

''I might,'' Nikki responded thoughtfully. ''But first let me ask you something. Are you in love with her?''

''I care about her,'' he said.

''That's not the same, is it?''

''No. What's your point?''

''She's a good person, Enrique. Don't mess with her head.''

''For cripe's sake, Nikki, I am not messing with her head. I don't know where this is going. How am I supposed to find out, if she starts pushing me away?''

''Is that what she's doing?''

''It seems that way to me. She hasn't moved, but she's barely speaking to me. Did I do or say something to offend her?''

''You really are worried about this, aren't you?''

''Of course I am. That's why I called.''

''Okay then, here's the deal. I can't say for sure, but I think it has to do with your job. We talked a little about how spooked I was by Tom's career. Allie seemed to be pretty much in the same place about yours. Apparently she just woke up to the fact that you put your life on the line on a regular basis.''

''This is about my job?'' Ricky echoed incredulously.

''I can't be certain, but that's my guess.''

He groaned. He could fix a lot of things. He could talk his way out of just about anything. But what the hell was he supposed to do about his career? He loved his profession. It was who he was. Nikki had to be wrong. Just because she freaked out on a regular basis about Tom's job, she was probably projecting her own feelings onto Allie. He resolved to go straight to the source and he wouldn't wait until tomorrow. He'd do it tonight.

Allie came home to find the house lit by candles and dinner simmering on the stove. Picadillo, black beans and rice. She had a feeling they could thank Mrs. Wilder or Maria for the food. She was less certain about the candles.

Ricky wandered out of the bathroom just then, a towel wrapped around his waist, his chest and hair still damp from a shower. It was not an image conducive to peace of mind. Her already-shaky resolve to fight the attraction she felt for this man took a solid hit, especially when his lips curved slowly into that irresistible smile of his.

"Hi." He gestured toward his barely concealed body. "I thought I had the place to myself."

Allie swallowed hard and tried to feign a nonchalance she was far from feeling. "It is your house."

A storm began to brew in his eyes. "Don't go there, Allie."

"I just meant—"

"I know what you meant," he retorted, his expression fierce. He seemed to be fighting a losing battle with himself. "Look, I'll be out in a few minutes. Dinner's almost ready. There's a bottle of wine on the kitchen counter. Pour yourself a glass, if you'd like one.''

She was about to protest, to make an excuse and retreat to her room to avoid whatever unpredictable mood he was in, but she got the distinct impression he'd be infuriated if she tried.

"Thanks," she said instead. "I'll just put these papers away.''

She had to brush past him in the narrow corridor to reach her room. He stubbornly refused to budge. She could feel the heat emanating from his body as she inched past. He smelled of soap and shampoo and pure masculinity. If she'd been another kind of woman, she would have reached out and given that precariously knotted towel a sharp tug just to see what might follow. As it was, she fought the impulse and made a dash for her room.

Closing the door behind her, she leaned against it and gasped for breath. "Oh, my," she murmured. She was in trouble. Knee-deep and sinking fast. More trouble than she'd ever imagined.

Worse, she thought, Ricky knew it. He might have turned up in the hallway wearing nothing but a towel and a smile by accident, but he'd lingered on purpose, enjoying her discomfort.

Why? That was what she wanted to know. What perversity had made him stand there and deliberately taunt her? Hadn't she been doing her best to steer clear of him ever since they'd gone on that double date with Tom and Nikki? Hadn't she practically told him by her actions that she considered them to be nothing more than casual roommates?

Hadn't she been lying through her teeth…to herself as well as him? She sighed heavily. She might as well admit it. She wanted Ricky Wilder, wanted him as she had never wanted another man, had never even been tempted by another man.

But he'd been right to warn her off. It would be a disaster. He was a flirt and a scoundrel, who took nothing very seriously except his work. She was serious and intense. When she finally got around to having a relationship, she intended for it to matter, for it to last. If that wasn't a doomed combination, what was?

She sighed again. She knew perfectly well that she couldn't hide out in her room. Ricky had already warned her against that. Surely she could spend an evening with him without acting on all of these raging impulses he stirred in her. She just had to get a grip and remember who he was, who *she* was.

When she finally emerged and headed for the kitchen, she was relieved that he wasn't there. She poured herself a glass of red wine and took a sip. Warmth cascaded through her. She felt better at once. Braver. She took another sip, then warned herself that continuing down that particular path would be folly.

She moved to the stove, lifted the lid on the picadillo and stirred the mixture of meat and spices, savoring the rich scent. Suddenly she felt Ricky's hand in the middle of her back. Her gaze shot up and met his as he leaned around her to check on the simmering pot of black beans. She couldn't seem to catch her breath.

"Hungry?" he inquired mildly, stepping back and pouring his own glass of wine.

Allie's pulse scrambled. Every sense was on full

alert, and all he cared about was food. That ought to tell her something.

"Starved," she said, proud that she managed to get the word out without choking.

"Me, too. Have a seat. I'll fix our plates."

Allie sat, because her knees were threatening to buckle anyway. Ricky put a full plate in front of her, set one at his own place, then dimmed the lights, leaving the room bathed in the glow of half a dozen candles.

Allie automatically tasted the food, but it might as well have been sawdust. She had to fight the urge to cast surreptitious glances at the man seated opposite her. Something was going on here that she didn't understand. His solicitous behavior, the candles, that little scene in the hallway, all of it pointed toward a man intent on seduction. Not that she had a lot of experience in that area, but she was pretty sure this wasn't the way casual roommates behaved.

She could let the evening take its own course or she could ask a few questions and take charge of it herself. She'd vowed a long time ago not to let circumstances control her life. The next few minutes might be awkward, especially if she'd gotten it all wrong, but at least she would know.

"Ricky?"

He regarded her with a questioning expression.

"What's going on here?" she asked.

"We're having dinner."

"Besides that?"

His lips twitched ever so slightly, but his eyes were serious as they clashed with hers. "What makes you think something's going on?"

"You." She gestured toward the candles. "This."

"You have a problem with the ambiance?"

"I don't have a problem with it," she said, not even trying to hide her exasperation. "Not exactly."

"What then?"

She wanted to smack the innocent expression off his face. She thought maybe a little bluntness would do the job.

"Are you trying to seduce me?" she asked.

This time his lips curved into a full-blown grin. "Yes," he said, taking the wind out of her sails.

Allie stared at him, openmouthed. She hadn't expected him to admit it. Now that he had, what was she supposed to say? What was she supposed to do? Tell him to forget it? Get all huffy and indignant and stalk away from the table? Out of the house, she corrected. She would have to get very far away, if she was to change the course he'd set.

The trouble was, her breath seemed to have lodged in her throat. Her body was shouting, "Hip hip hurray!" and all but daring her to say yes.

"Do you have a problem with that?" Ricky inquired lazily.

Allie swallowed hard and tried to muster up the protest that her brain assured her was appropriate.

"No," she whispered finally. "No, I don't have a problem with that."

His grin spread. "Good."

He reached over, picked up her hand and pressed a kiss to her palm. A shudder rolled through her.

"Eat," he advised. "You're going to need the energy."

Allie wanted to make some clever, snippy little

comment about his ego, but she didn't. She picked up her fork and ate. It was hard to concentrate on beans and rice, though, when all she could think about was dessert.

# Chapter Thirteen

Ricky had taken a huge risk when he'd admitted to Allie that he intended to seduce her. He almost expected her to bolt from the room. For a minute, in fact, she'd looked as if she wanted to.

Then, to his amazement and relief, she met his gaze evenly and said, "Yes." He hadn't tasted another bite of food after that.

Still, he'd been determined not to rush her. He wanted to give her a little time to get used to the idea. He even wanted her to have time to change her mind, though he was pretty sure he would die if she did.

They even managed to carry on a conversation during the rest of the meal. He couldn't recall now what it had been about, but it had seemed brilliant enough at the time.

Finally, when the table had been carefully cleared

and the dishes dutifully done, she looked up at him, her heart in her eyes, and asked, "This seduction of yours, is it going to be tonight?"

Ricky swallowed hard, fighting the need that made him want to reach out and claim her. "Are you still okay with that?"

He lasted until she gave him the slightest nod and then his lips settled against hers. He'd lectured himself for the past hour to go slowly. He'd assured himself that he could.

But one taste of her had him reevaluating. Need slammed through him, hot and urgent. Still he kept the kiss light, persuasive and coaxing, rather than demanding. She whimpered against his mouth, clearly wanting more. His blood roared in his ears, insisting that he go along with her.

He fought that urge and all the others that tugged at him, settling instead for the sweet torment of a slow burn. Oh, he was on fire for her, all right. He'd never known anyone like her, a woman who offered everything. The complete surrender was as unexpected as it was exciting. It washed away all of the doubts that had made him hold back for weeks now. He promised himself he would make sure she didn't regret her decision, not tonight, not ever.

His mouth was still locked with hers when he scooped her up and cradled her against his chest. Even as small as his house was, it seemed to take forever, but he reached his bedroom eventually after stopping along the way to blow out each and every candle. The firefighter in him was unwilling to trade safety for ambience. Then he closed the door, leaving a disappointed Shadow on the other side. He heard a whimper as he carried Allie to the bed, then the thump of the dog's body settling against the door.

He lowered Allie gently to the bed. "Allie, are you sure?" he asked one more time as he stood staring down at her.

Dazed, dreamy eyes met his. "About what?"

"About this?" he said. "Making love?"

She stretched languidly, then scooted onto her knees and put her hands on either side of his face. Her gaze was clear, her expression determined. "Very sure," she assured him, then slanted her mouth across his and plunged her tongue inside in a way that removed all trace of doubt.

Ricky felt something inside him shatter. Later he would have to figure out what the sensation was, but for now he knew only that touching Allie was more thrilling than anything he'd ever experienced, in bed or out. He couldn't seem to get enough of the feel of her soft skin as he slowly removed first her blouse, then her bra, noting as he did that it was one of the sexy ones he'd picked out for her. Then he feasted on the sight of her bared breasts, the dusky peaks, the pebble-hard nipples. For now it was enough just to drink in the sight. Touching, tasting would come later.

When he'd satisfied himself with that vision, he slid the zipper of her slacks down, then trailed his fingers along satiny flesh until he reached the silky barrier of her panties. He paused, then moved on. Her eyes widened with surprise, then pleasure as he touched the hot, slick core of her. She gasped when he stripped away panties and touched the same place with his tongue. Her hips rose off the bed as she strained toward his touch and toward an elusive release.

"Not yet, *querida*. Not yet," he murmured, shifting his attention to her breasts, which were peaked with arousal. Her cries pleased him, but he wanted more. He wanted to give her an experience she would never forget, never equal.

She stirred restlessly when he pulled away. She reached for him, but he slipped out of reach, letting the sensations die to a simmer before stirring them back up again with a slow caress, a tender kiss, a deliberate slide of expert fingers deep inside her. She bucked against him, once again begging for a release he refused.

There was a sheen of perspiration on her body, an undeniable tension to her muscles. He felt that tension mirrored in his own body, which was hard and aching from the long denial.

"Please," she whispered, her voice hoarse with need.

Ricky guessed that she was at the end of her rope, *knew* that he was. He slipped out of the shirt that she had tried to remove, then shed his jeans. Her avid gaze fell on his arousal. She reached out tentatively, then drew one finger along the hard shaft. Ricky thought he might explode. He doubted she understood the danger, so he guided her hand to safer territory, but even her touch against his chest had him tensing with desire.

Once again he began to explore her body, partly to distract her from her own exploration, partly to begin the last slow climb to the peak he'd denied her time and again tonight. Satisfied at last that she was at the top, at the edge, he knelt between her legs and entered her in one fast, urgent thrust.

She shattered at once, her contractions hard and deep. He waited, perfectly still, until they slowed, and then he began the age-old rhythm that would take them both to the top yet again. She cried out as the sensations tore through her, and this time, with her cries echoing in his head and her slick heat surrounding him, he joined her in a shuddering release.

His breath came back eventually. His heartbeat quieted to a normal pace, but he couldn't bring himself to move. Something had happened to him tonight, something he'd never expected, never imagined. He'd made love, in every sense of the phrase. He couldn't deny it. He'd had a lot of experience with sex and none with making love. He could tell the difference. This, *this,* had been something special, something he would never get enough of, something he was reluctant to end.

He rolled over, bringing Allie with him, still joined in the most intimate way possible, still bound by that inexplicable bond that he'd wondered about but had spent a lifetime doubting.

She sighed heavily and stirred. When she would have moved away from him, he held her tight. He didn't want to talk, didn't want to gaze into her eyes to see if she felt the same way. He put his life on the line all the time without a second thought, but he didn't want to risk this moment, this magic. Damn, she had him thinking like a blasted poet, all soft and mushy and romantic. It wasn't his style. Permanence sure as hell wasn't his style.

But that's exactly what he wanted. Forever. He finally dared a glance at Allie's face. He saw satisfaction there, maybe even joy, but he thought he also detected a glint of determination in her eyes. He couldn't figure out what that was about, but something told him it couldn't possibly be good.

"Okay," he said warily. "What's on your mind?"

"The truth?"

"Always." Even when it hurt, and he was pretty sure this was going to.

"You're so good at this and I'm… Well, I'm not exactly experienced."

His mouth gaped. She needed reassurance? The woman who'd all but destroyed him? "Are you fishing for a compliment?" he asked.

"Of course not," she protested. "I'm trying to be honest."

"Allie, if you were any better at this, we'd collapse from exhaustion."

Her lips tilted up, but the smile faded before it could blossom. "But all those other women…"

"There are no other women. Not like you."

She continued to regard him doubtfully. Ricky couldn't think of any other way to persuade her except to show her in lingering, tormenting detail.

He wasn't entirely sure how convincing he was, but at least when he was through, she was way too breathless to argue. Good thing, too, because he really, really needed some time to figure out what he was going to do about the discovery he'd just made that he was falling in love with Allie Matthews.

Allie was pretty sure her brain must have been starved for oxygen while she was under her collapsed house. Not only had she moved in with a virtual stranger, but now, a scant few weeks later, she was sharing his bed. Maybe Ricky had been right after all, and she was incapable of clear thought. She was certainly behaving more impetuously than was her habit.

The proof? Tonight's lovemaking had happened after she had very firmly told herself that Ricky Wilder was not the kind of man she wanted in her life. She wanted someone solid and dependable, someone who didn't have a history of loving and leaving every woman he'd ever known.

Okay, she couldn't exactly accuse Ricky of not being solid and dependable, could she? After all, he had saved her life.

But he was also an outrageous flirt, a fact confirmed by everyone who knew him and that he himself had never bothered to deny. Despite his reassurances that she more than measured up to all those other women in his life, he hadn't exactly given her any reason to believe their relationship would be any more lasting than the others had been.

Moreover—and here was the real problem—he didn't think twice about putting his life on the line. Every time she thought of what he did for a living, she shuddered. She wanted a man who would be home every night, whose greatest risk was negotiating I-95 on his way to work. Life could be unpredictable enough without deliberately taking chances. She knew that better than anyone.

As if to prove her point, Ricky suddenly shifted away from her and reached for the phone. Allie glanced at the clock. It was the middle of the night. A ringing phone at two in the morning was never about something good. She tensed, watching his face for clues about what was being said on the other end of the line.

"I'll be there," he said at last, casting an apologetic look her way.

"What is it?" she asked, when he had hung up.

"An earthquake in El Salvador. It happened about an hour ago. The epicenter was only a few miles from San Salvador. It's a bad one, Allie. We have to go."

She swallowed hard against the longing to tell him to stay. This was his job. He had no choice. She knew that, but of all nights, the disaster couldn't have come on a worse one. She felt bereft as he moved out of her arms and began quickly and methodically getting ready to go, his mind already clicking through some long-established mental checklist.

She huddled in the bed, sheets drawn up to her chin as she watched him transform himself from lover to professional rescue worker in the blink of an eye. The brisk movements and grim expression banished any signs of the tenderness she had experienced in his arms just moments before.

He was showered and ready in minutes. He paused by the bed.

"I'm sorry. If there was any choice, I would stay here with you."

"I understand," she assured him. And it was true. She did. But that didn't seem to stop the knot of fear that was tightening in her belly or the dull thud of her heart or the images of him broken and bloody that formed in her head.

"Will you be okay?" he asked. "I mean with this." He gestured toward the tangle of sheets, still warm from their frenzied lovemaking.

"We'll talk about it when you get back," she said. "I know you need to go. Take care of yourself."

"Always," he said as he touched his lips to hers in a fleeting, distracted kiss.

His head was already somewhere else. She could tell, and it hurt somewhere deep inside to know that he had left her behind even before walking out of the room.

He stopped at the door. "I'll get word to you when I can."

"How?" she asked, thoroughly frustrated by the realization that he couldn't just pick up the phone and call her on a whim as he might any other woman.

"It's okay," he soothed, clearly picking up on her anxiety. "A lot's going to depend on phone lines there being up, but I'll think of something. I'll get word to the clinic and have someone give you a message, or I'll have Maria or my mother come by."

She nodded, relieved that she wouldn't have to endure the days or even weeks without knowing what was happening or whether he was safe. "Thank you."

As he opened the door, she saw Shadow standing, ready and alert, as if he sensed that he, too, was on duty. And then they were gone.

Her spirits sank the minute the two of them disappeared from sight. She crept out of bed, tugged on Ricky's shirt just to be surrounded by the scent of him, then went into the living room to stare out the window as his car pulled away. She watched until the taillights vanished in the darkness.

More than she ever had before, she regretted her inability to hear. She desperately wanted to be able to call someone like Nikki, who would share her anxiety, who could commiserate with this sense of fear and abandonment. The latter, of course, was worse because of the timing of that fateful call. It had ripped Ricky out of her arms, taken him from their bed just as they were discovering the overwhelming tide of sweet passion that could carry them away. She had waited so long for that moment, convinced herself it might never happen. To have the joy of it cut short was a painful reminder that a life with Ricky would always be uncertain, that it could be cut short in the blink of an eye.

Because she couldn't sleep anyway, she showered, dressed and settled in front of the TV in the living room, tuned in CNN and watched the reports just beginning to come out of the ravaged city of San Salvador. The reports contained raw footage just sent in via satellite, the pictures graphic and uncensored. Allie had no idea what information accompanied the images, because the anchor was off camera. She just knew that her heart climbed into her throat when she tried to imagine Ricky arriving in the midst of that devastation.

She was almost relieved when it was time to leave for work. She desperately needed the break, but the first thing Gina asked when she saw her was whether Ricky had had to fly to El Salvador.

Allie nodded. "He got a call about two in the morning."

Gina studied her with a penetrating look. "How do you feel about that?"

"Scared," she admitted.

"Maybe it will get easier once you've been through a few disasters."

Allie considered that, then shook her head. ''I don't think so.''

''Is there anything I can do for you to make it easier?''

''I can't think of anything, but he might call here to let me know how things are going.''

''I'll get you the second he does,'' Gina promised. ''Maybe you should get the same phone equipment at home, so he can call you there. You had it at your place, didn't you?''

Similar to e-mail, the equipment transmitted the caller's written words on a screen for the benefit of the deaf. It also had a blinking light to indicate when a call was coming in. It was a remarkable advancement.

''I had it before the storm, but I was going to wait till I got settled before replacing it.''

''I think it's too important,'' Gina chided, signing emphatically. ''You need to be able to communicate, not just with him but with other people, as well. Let me see if I can't make arrangements for it to get set up.''

''Thank you,'' she said, grateful for the nudging. She realized she had been resisting installing the equipment at Ricky's because she didn't want it to seem as if she was settling in on a permanent basis. Now, though, she was sure he would understand how vital it was. He would probably even be grateful that she wouldn't be cut off from the outside world when he wasn't there.

Over the next week, her life took on a surreal quality. When she wasn't at work, she was glued to the television news, hoping to catch a glimpse of Ricky.

A local station had a news crew on the scene and often featured interviews with the rescue crew from Miami.

Some nights Nikki did come over and they watched together. On other nights Maria or her mother dropped by, sometimes with messages from Ricky.

Allie was grateful to all of them, not only for the company, but for the information they were able to pass along.

"This must be so hard on you," Maria said. "I know it's driving Ricky crazy not to be able to talk to you. Usually he's totally focused, when he's on one of these assignments, but now when he calls he has a million and one questions about you. I've never known him to care enough about a woman that she even crosses his mind while he's working."

Maria grinned. "I think that's wonderful, by the way. It's about time he found a woman who could put up with him and maybe put a little balance into his life."

But what if I can't? Allie wanted to ask, but didn't. How could she explain to Ricky's sister that she wasn't at all sure she could live with what he did for a living. Her own near tragedy was still too fresh in her mind to allow her to be complacent about the dangers he was intentionally facing every single second of every exhausting day. The possibility that she might be a dangerous distraction was far from reassuring.

She was able to voice her fear to Nikki, though. She saw the same tight lines of tension in her friend's face as she saw reflected in the mirror when she was dressing in the morning.

"It never gets any easier," Nikki said, tearing her gaze away from the television when the news switched to another story.

"What are you going to do?" Allie asked her. "You were thinking of going back to Tom before this happened, weren't you?"

Nikki nodded, her expression miserable. "If I thought for one single second that I could get through the rest of my life and never think about Tom again, I would move on, find some nice, boring accountant and raise a family. Unfortunately, Tom is the man I love, the man I've always loved. I could marry somebody else and move to Alaska and I still think I'd panic every time I heard about a natural disaster."

She shrugged. "Given all that, I might as well marry the man and have whatever time together that God grants us." Her expression brightened. "One of these days he's going to be too old to do this for a living. He'll be around the house, underfoot, and I'll be the one grumbling about the good old days when he was halfway around the world taking risks."

Allie tried to imagine such a time, but couldn't. She would thank her lucky stars to have Rick underfoot. Whatever adjustments that would require were bound to be better than this fear that hadn't left her since the minute he walked out of the house.

He had been away for two endless weeks, during which she had never gotten remotely used to his absence, nor to accepting the reason for it with any sort of equanimity. It was the most frustrating experience of her life. It was also all the proof she needed that she was with the wrong man. There was no way she could live with this sort of unnerving uncertainty.

But when she drove into the driveway on Saturday

morning after a trip to the grocery store, she saw his car parked in front of the garage, and her heart began to race. Then the front door opened, and he stepped outside. She flew out of the car and straight into his arms.

Relief and desire replaced tension and exhaustion. His mouth on hers was eager and demanding, his touch reassuring. In the heat of their reunion, she managed to forget all about her reservations.

It was hours later before she remembered the groceries. Laughing, she retrieved once-frozen food ruined by the heat, bread that had been baked a little too long by the sun and milk that had been spoiled. It seemed like a small price to pay for having Ricky back and for sharing his bed.

"Gina's getting the phone equipment so I won't be so cut off the next time you go away," she told him as she warmed up leftovers from the meal Maria had dropped off the night before.

"I was thinking about that," Ricky said, his expression thoughtful.

"Any ideas?" she asked.

"We could get a couple of computers and chat online. That would work. Or at least we'd be able to e-mail each other. I just know we have to do something," he said, his gaze locked with hers, his hands settled on her waist as the food simmered unnoticed on the stove behind her. "This was the most frustrating two weeks I've ever had on the job. Not being able to check in with you directly was making me crazy."

It helped to know that his frustration had been as great as her own.

But that night as Allie snuggled next to him, his

arm draped across her stomach, her hand resting against his chest, the sense of relief she felt at having him back safely took a back seat to the awareness that there would always be a next time and then another and another. All of the fear came flooding back, robbing her of the little bit of serenity she'd been able to reclaim.

She was quiet on Sunday. She spent most of the day inventing chores that took her away from the house, so she could be alone to think. It was ironic really. Being alone had grated on her nerves for the past two weeks, but now she sought out the solitude.

That night Ricky called her on it.

"What's up, Allie? You've been avoiding me all day."

"I've needed to think."

"About?"

She returned his gaze, feeling miserable and torn, but knowing what she had to do. "Us," she admitted finally. "This won't work, Ricky. It can't."

He stared at her in openmouthed astonishment. "What exactly are you saying—that you want to end this?"

"Yes," she told him. "I think it would be best if I move out."

His expression turned stoic. "Mind if I ask why?"

"It's because of what you do," she admitted. "For the past two weeks I have been almost sick with worry. I don't think I could do that for the rest of my life, just sit here and wait while you risk your life."

"The rest of your life?" he asked, looking incredulous. "You've done it exactly *once*. You and I, we're just starting to find our way. We don't know what's going to happen between us a week from now. Don't you think it's a little soon to start worrying about the rest of our lives?''

She was taken aback by the suggestion that she'd been unfair, that she'd leaped way too far into the future. ''I just know how I feel,'' she said defensively. ''Why drag it out?''

His expression darkened. ''This is Nikki's doing, isn't it? She spent too much time here while I was gone, filling your head with nonsense about how dangerous my job is.''

''It's not nonsense,'' Allie said. ''And don't blame Nikki. I felt this way before the last trip even happened. The trip just crystallized what I was feeling. You're the kind of man who obviously needs to live life on the edge. I'm not knocking you for making that choice. What you do is important and you're incredibly brave. I'm just saying I can't live with it.''

''And you know that, after I've been on one assignment? It doesn't take much to scare you off, does it?''

She saw the mounting frustration in his expression, caught the flare of anger building in his eyes, but she couldn't figure out a way to make him understand.

''I lived through a disaster all too recently,'' she began.

''You survived, thanks to me,'' he pointed out.

''Yes, thanks to you,'' she said quietly. ''That's why I admire what you do. I respect you for it. I'm grateful that there are men like you who are willing to take the risks, but nobody knows better than I do just how great that risk is. The minute you walked out that door, I was back under that rubble again, trapped in the dark, terrified that I was going to die there. I know that with time the memories of that will dim, but how can they if I have to relive them over and over every time you go on an assignment?''

His anger visibly faded as her words sank in. He reached for her and pulled her close, his expression shattered. ''I'm sorry. When you put it like that, it makes a horrible kind of sense to me. I hate it, but it's true.''

She lifted her gaze to his. ''I have to move out,'' she told him. ''I don't see any other choice.''

A sigh shuddered through him. She could feel it as her cheek rested against his chest, but he didn't argue.

Much later, when he released her, she saw only sorrow and regret in his eyes.

''If you can wait until tomorrow evening, I'll help you find a place of your own,'' he offered.

''You don't need to do that,'' she said, pretty sure she would find it unbearable to have his presence indelibly linked to whatever house or apartment she rented.

''Let me do that much,'' he said, his expression set stubbornly.

Allie finally, reluctantly, nodded agreement because it clearly meant a lot to him. She just had to keep reminding herself that when the apartment hunt was over, she would have the rest of her life to get over the pain of walking away. But how long would it be before she knew if day-to-day serenity was a fair trade for losing a lifetime with the man she was beginning to love?

## Chapter Fourteen

Jane was beside herself when she heard what Allie intended to do. Apparently Ricky had filled her in, because she turned up at the clinic at lunchtime with a determined glint in her eye and a picnic hamper filled with Allie's favorite foods.

"Why are you here?" Allie asked warily.

"To talk some sense into you."

"Why are you siding with Ricky on this without even listening to how I feel?"

"I am on your side, always, which is why I'm here. I doubt, though, that there's anything you could say that would convince me that you're not throwing away a real chance at happiness."

She reached in the hamper and drew out a container of pasta salad. "Here, eat some of this."

Under her friend's watchful gaze, Allie took the salad and a fork and automatically began to eat.

There were bits of ham, cheese and bell peppers in the salad, just the way she liked it, just the way her mother had always made it. It was comfort food and Jane knew it.

"It's very good. Thank you."

"Now try this," Jane said, handing over a freshly baked brownie. "I brought more for the rest of the staff."

"They'll love you forever. Your brownies are always a big hit around here."

"I'm delighted to hear it," Jane said, though her expression remained grimly determined.

Allie took her time savoring the rich, moist brownie, which was filled with chocolate chips and walnuts, because she sensed that the minute Jane was satisfied that she was well fed, she was going to launch into a lecture. That was her way. She figured people were always more sensible with a full stomach.

Sure enough, the minute Allie had eaten the last crumb, Jane said, "Now then, let's get back to this lunacy about you moving out of Ricky's."

Allie bristled. "Telling me I'm nuts is not likely to make me receptive to whatever else you have to say."

"I call 'em as I see 'em," Jane retorted, hands on hips. The tough-woman effect was somewhat lessened by the pink sneakers and flowered baseball cap. "Live with it."

A grin tugged at Allie's lips, despite her determination not to be swayed by anything her former neighbor had to say.

"Look, I know Ricky must have called you. Did

he mention why I thought it was important to get my own place?''

"Well, of course he did. He even said he could understand it.''

"Then there's not a problem, is there?''

"Well, I don't understand it,'' Jane said. "I've seen the two of you together. If ever two people belonged with each other, it's you. If your mother were here, she'd tell you the same thing. Since she's not, I figure it's up to me.''

"Actually, my mother doesn't have an opinion about this, one way or the other. She's not aware that my roommate is a man.''

Jane stared incredulously. "How on earth can that be? Don't the two of you talk? Hasn't Ricky ever answered the phone?''

"Actually she prefers letters,'' Allie admitted stiffly.

"Why because she doesn't want that phone equipment around to remind her that you're deaf?''

"Something like that.''

Jane muttered something. Allie figured it was just as well she hadn't been able to see her lips. She doubted it had been complimentary. She tried to head off any more discussion.

"Jane—''

"Enough about your mother. I'll keep my opinion to myself about that,'' she said, cutting off Allie's comment. "Now let me share something with you, Allie. I was married for thirty years. You never met my husband, but he was a lot like Ricky. He had a sense of honor and commitment to other people. We met when we were teenagers, before I had any idea that he was going to be a policeman. I was so proud of him the day he graduated from the police academy, but there wasn't a single day after that when I wasn't terrified that he might not come home to me.'' She leveled a look straight into Allie's eyes, then added pointedly, ''Not one single day.''

Allie got the message. By comparison, Ricky's risks were far less frequent. Allie was behaving like a coward in not accepting the risks as a small price to pay for a love that could bring her joy. Unfortunately, she also knew how the story ended.

''In the end your worst fears were realized,'' she reminded Jane gently.

''Yes, they were,'' she admitted, her eyes swimming with tears even after twenty years without her beloved husband. ''He died in the line of duty, and I was devastated. But at least I knew I'd had thirty years with the best man on the face of the earth. If I had given in to my fears, I would have had nothing. No memories to cherish. No children or grandchildren. Ricky is a rare man, my dear. He's compassionate and brave. And he deserves a woman who can appreciate that.''

''I do,'' Allie said fiercely. ''That's what makes this so hard. I know what a wonderful man he is.''

''Then don't let the fear win,'' Jane advised. She gathered up the empty food containers, then patted Allie's cheek. ''Think about it. That's all I ask. And listen to your heart.''

Allie had no problem at all hearing her heart. What terrified her was that it was going to wind up broken.

When Ricky came home and found Allie packing, he told himself it was for the best. He wasn't after permanence, never had been. Helping her to look for a new place to live would have just dragged out an already awkward situation.

"Where are you going? Did you find a place this afternoon?" he asked.

She avoided looking directly at him when she answered. "I'm going to stay with a friend temporarily."

Since there hadn't been a friend who could take her in when she left the hospital, he couldn't help wondering who it might be.

"Mind telling me who this friend is?" he inquired casually. "In case I need to reach you or forward your mail or something."

Her expression turned defiant. "Maria."

Ricky felt his blood begin to heat. "You're moving in with *my sister?* How the hell did that happen?" And how was he supposed to get over Allie, if she was living in the midst of his damn family?

"She came over, found me packing and refused to let me go to a motel."

"Well, isn't that just downright sisterly of her," he muttered bitterly.

Allie sank down on the side of the bed, her defiance slipping away. "I'm sorry. I know this is awkward. I tried to get out of it, but you know Maria," she said with a resigned shrug.

"I most certainly do," he said grimly, imagining exactly how the conversation had gone. Allie might be a more-than-even match for him, but she was definitely not equal to his big sister when Maria was on a mission. The only question was what she considered that mission to be. He whirled around and headed for the phone. He wasn't especially surprised when his sister answered on the first ring.

"Expecting my call?" he asked sarcastically, grateful that the portable phone allowed him to pace.

"Something like that."

"What are you up to?"

"You're not the only one in the family who can help a friend in need," she retorted. "Allie needed a place to stay. We have a guest room. I offered to let her use it."

"Why not let her move into a motel or her own apartment, the way she intended?"

"I could ask you the same question. Isn't that how she wound up at your house in the first place?"

Frustration coiled deep inside him. "Maria, you're not helping."

She chuckled at that. "I may not be helping you, but I'm pretty sure I'm doing Allie a favor. Come to think of it, I'm also pretty sure that one day you'll thank me."

"For what?"

"For not letting her get away."

"It's not as if she was planning to move to California," he pointed out. "I could have found her if I'd wanted to."

"But this way you won't have to waste time looking," Maria said cheerfully. "Gotta run. The kids want to watch a video. Tell Allie I'll be expecting her over here in time for dinner. You can come, too, if you want."

"Don't expect me."

"Suit yourself," she said blandly.

He sighed heavily.

"Enrique?"

"Yes, what?"

"I love you."

"I know that."

"So does Allie."

He thought he had known that, too, but the past twenty-four hours had made him question it. He hung up on his sister and went in search of his soon-to-depart houseguest...his lover, he reminded himself. He found her in the foyer, surrounded by her luggage. Shadow sat at her feet, watching her quizzically.

He noted that she hadn't acquired all that much while living with him. Just some clothes, a few essentials...and his heart.

"Did Maria answer all your questions?" she inquired politely.

"Not to my satisfaction, but she tried."

"Well, I'll be going now."

"Allie, you don't have to do this."

Her sad gaze met his, then darted away. "Yes," she said softly. "I do."

Ricky didn't know what else to say. He couldn't tell her the one thing she wanted to hear, that he would quit his job and do something less risky. Instead he just picked up her luggage and carried it out to her car, watched as she got settled behind the wheel.

"Since you'll be at Maria's, I imagine we'll bump into each other once in a while," he said.

"I'll try to make sure that doesn't happen," she said, gazing up at him through the open window. "I don't want you to feel uncomfortable about visiting your own sister."

"I won't be uncomfortable," he insisted. Just miserable.

"Whatever. Thank you for everything."

"You're welcome," he said, chafing at the exchange that made them sound like polite strangers.

Because he couldn't stand the distance a second longer, he bent down and captured her lips in a greedy, demanding kiss meant to remind her—remind them both—of what they were giving up.

She looked shaken when he finally pulled away, but that didn't stop her from reaching for the key to start the car, turning it with fingers that visibly trembled. Then she hit the power button to close the window between them, shifted the car into reverse and eased away from him, distancing herself from his life.

Watching her go was the hardest thing Ricky had ever had to do. The instant the car disappeared from sight he knew that he was making the worst mistake he'd ever made.

He shouted her name, then ran to the end of the driveway, Shadow barking alongside him. He slammed his fist into the mailbox in frustration when he realized what a wasted gesture the shout had been. How could he even tell her he loved her, when he didn't know the right words and she couldn't hear them even if he did?

He could think of only one person who would totally understand what he was going through. He called Tom, only to learn that Nikki was with him.

"She's agreed to think about getting married again," Tom exulted. "I really think we're going to make it work this time. She's dropped that whole thing about me working for her dad."

"What have you had to give up in return?"

"I've promised that I'll think about changing jobs in five years. I'll be thirty-five then. I'll probably be ready to do something that doesn't take me on the road so much, especially if we have kids.''

"Sounds like you've got it all worked out," Ricky said, fighting to hide the bitterness in his own voice. It wasn't Tom's fault that *his* love life was working out while Ricky's was going to hell.

"Why did you call, Enrique? You don't sound so good."

"It's nothing. You enjoy your evening with Nikki, okay? You two deserve it." He hung up before he could dump all of his problems on his friend.

He didn't miss the irony that the woman he'd blamed for instilling her own fears into Allie had somehow managed to get past those very same fears. Well, good for her, he thought sourly. And good for Tom.

Since he refused to wallow in self-pity, he changed clothes and went into the garage, picked up his hedge clippers and began to chop the hell out of an over-grown bougainvillea.

He was still at it two hours later when his mother arrived. She took one look at him and at the practically denuded flowering shrub and yanked the clippers away from him.

"Are you *loco?*" she demanded.

Ricky had the distinct impression that she was questioning more than his rampage with the clippers.

"Leave it alone, Mama." He stalked past her and headed for the kitchen. He pulled out a beer, popped the tab and chugged down a long, thirst-quenching swallow.

Hands on hips, she stood in the doorway and scowled at him. "I taught you better than that."

"Better than what?"

"To turn your back on a woman like Allie."

"I didn't turn my back on her. It was her choice to move out."

"But you let her go."

"What choice did I have? She said she worried too much about my safety, that she couldn't live with the thought of something happening to me."

"You think I don't understand such fear?" his mother said.

"But you've never asked me to give up the career I love."

"Of course not. Did she ask such a thing?"

"No. She just packed up and bailed."

"Then get her back."

Ricky regarded her with mounting frustration. "How do you suggest I do that?"

"If you can't figure it out, then you are no son of mine."

He wasn't particularly impressed with the threat. "You've been disowning me my whole life, every time I do something to displease you. I don't take it seriously anymore."

She muttered a string of Spanish epithets he hadn't even realized his mother knew. He stared at her in shock. She scowled right back at him.

"Well, what do you expect?" she snapped. "Your father and I agree that Allie is the best thing that ever happened to you and you let her walk away. Did you even fight to keep her here? Did you tell her how you feel?"

"I don't know how to tell her any more clearly than I have."

His mother's gaze narrowed. "Then you do realize that you love her?"

"Of course," he retorted. "It's the words I don't know, the ones that will convince her."

"Convince her of what? That she means the world to you, that you want to take care of her and love her, have babies with her?"

"Yes, those words."

She rolled her eyes. "What is wrong with the ones you have just spoken to me?"

"You said the words," he pointed out. "I just agreed."

She stared at him, visibly exasperated. "Saints protect me, do I have to propose for you, too?"

"If you want there to be a wedding, it might not be a bad idea."

She cuffed him gently upside the head. "You are a man. A foolish one, but a man, nonetheless. Tell the woman what is in your heart. She will hear you well enough."

Overnight he thought about what his mother had said. Would mere words really make a difference? Hadn't he tried already, only to be rebuffed? He scoffed at the idea that one try was enough, given what was at stake. His mother was right. He owed it to both of them to try again...and again, if necessary.

On Saturday morning he decided to brave his sister's likely amusement, his nephews' interference and his brother-in-law's taunts. He arrived at Maria's to find the entire family gathered around the breakfast table, Allie included. She and Ramón were having a heated discussion about baseball versus soccer. Apparently Allie was a huge Florida Marlins fan, something Ricky hadn't discovered while she stayed with him though the T-shirt she'd worn when he rescued her should have been a clue. How many more things were there that he didn't know about her?

"Pull up a chair," his brother-in-law offered. "I think there's enough batter left for a few pancakes. Maria thought you might be by."

"Did she now?" Ricky asked, casting a scowl in his sister's direction.

"Just optimistic," she said with a smile. She clapped her hands together to get the attention of her sons. "Boys, outside. Let the grown-ups have some peace and quiet."

The boys didn't waste a second scrambling to get away. If only getting rid of Maria and her husband would be as simple, Ricky thought wistfully. Unfortunately, they poured themselves second cups of coffee and settled back to watch him eat his pancakes while they waited to see what transpired between him and Allie. She looked as if she wanted desperately to bolt right behind his nephews.

Ricky studied her. She didn't look any more rested than she had when she'd left his place. Apparently, the serenity she'd craved had remained elusive.

"Are you settling in okay?" he inquired.

"Maria and her family have been very gracious," she said.

"That's good. How's work?"

"Fine."

"And Jane?"

"She's doing okay. I'm surprised you haven't talked to her."

"I'm planning to see her tomorrow. In fact, I've invited her to Mama's for Sunday dinner."

That got a reaction. "You have?"

"I thought you might want to come, too."

She looked tempted, but she shook her head. ''No, thanks.''

Maria heaved an impatient sigh, then turned to her husband. ''Obviously, they don't intend to get into any of the good stuff as long as you and I are in the room. Want to take the kids and go to the beach?''

''Sounds good to me,'' Benny agreed, grinning at Ricky. ''But you're going to owe us.''

''I usually do,'' Ricky said.

As soon as they were gone, he faced Allie. ''I've missed you.''

''Ricky, don't. Please.''

''Don't what? Don't be honest?''

''Not when there's no point to it.''

''There's always a point to being truthful. Before you throw away what we have, I want you to see the whole picture.''

''What whole picture?'' she asked warily.

''I'll admit that it comes as a shock to me, but I see a future for the two of us. I see us married, living in my place for now, but eventually in someplace bigger, maybe with a pool in back. I see us having a family. Maybe two boys and a girl. I see us growing old together.''

Suddenly she was blinking back tears. ''Stop,'' she pleaded. ''That's the part of the picture I can't see.''

He knew precisely where she had stumbled. ''Getting old together?''

''Yes. Every time I try to get past the here and now, to see into the future, I see something terrible happening to take you away from me.''

He tried to think of some way to put her fears to rest, but the truth was it could happen exactly as she feared. But wasn't life filled with that kind of uncertainty. He could get killed in an accident on I-95 as easily as he could doing his job.

"Life doesn't come with guarantees no matter what you do for a living," he pointed out. "I love you. Doesn't that mean anything?"

"It means everything," she said, but her eyes were still filled with sorrow. "But I can't marry you. I need someone who will always come home to me."

"But I will," he insisted.

"You can't promise that, not and continue doing the job you love."

"The job that brought us together," he pointed out.

She touched a hand to his cheek. "And it is a part of who you are and why I love you," she said sadly. "But it's also the reason I can't marry you. I simply can't live with that kind of fear."

Ricky didn't begin to understand, but he saw the determined glint in her eyes and knew that she meant what she said. He leaned down and pressed a kiss to her lips, then to the dampness on her cheeks, before turning and walking away.

A week later, at the site of another earthquake, he took a dangerous misstep and found himself buried in rubble. Concrete and steel shifted precariously, slamming into flesh and bone. It was an uneven match. The pain was agonizing, but not nearly as agonizing as the realization that he was the one who'd been at fault, endangering not just himself, but others at the site.

He hadn't been concentrating, not the way he needed to. He wanted to blame Allie, blame the fact that he couldn't get her out of his head, but the truth was he'd been rushing, anxious to get the work over with so he could go back home again. He'd been entirely focused on proving to Allie that he would always come home.

Now it seemed, as he swam in and out of consciousness, he might have proved exactly the opposite. He had enough medical training to know that things weren't good. Blood was flowing from the injury to his head, which pounded like a jackhammer at the slightest movement. A shaft of metal had penetrated his thigh, too darned close to a major artery by the looks of it. He retched at the sight, then forced himself to take slow, deep breaths, head turned away.

He could hear Shadow's frantic barks, knew that Tom and the others would be conducting the slow, tedious excavation necessary to reach him where he was trapped.

As he drifted in and out of consciousness, he imagined what it must have been like for Allie to be trapped like this and terrified, her fate in the hands of strangers. It was little wonder that she didn't care to repeat the experience, albeit vicariously.

Even for him, knowing that his life was in the hands of experts whose skill was unquestionably the best, there was a sick feeling in the pit of his stomach that his luck might have run out. Trusting Tom and the other members of his crew didn't seem to figure into it, when he was too blasted close to bleeding to death, too much at risk of being crushed at any second.

Worse, he kept imagining Allie's reaction to the news. His frustration mounted with each second that dragged on, with each moment of uncertainty she must be facing. He hated himself for putting her through it, yet he knew if a choice had to be made, he would do it again. What he did was important, necessary work and he was good at it. Most of the time, anyway.

He had to resist the desperate desire to begin his own frantic excavation. For one thing, he knew he had to conserve his strength. For another, every movement caused blinding pain. He had to put his faith in the men he knew like brothers.

As he waited for help to come, he cursed his injuries, not because of the pain, but because Allie would see them as more proof that she had made the right decision. He cursed the fact that there were news crews on the scene to report every detail back home.

When the frustration and pain got to be too much, he concentrated on staying calm, staying alive. It wasn't just survival instinct that kept him going. It was Allie. He'd made her a promise and he had to fight with everything in him to be sure he kept it.

He was not going to die, buried in the very rubble from which he was supposed to rescue others, not now, not when he'd finally found the best possible reason for living: a woman he loved with all his heart.

## Chapter Fifteen

Allie hadn't been able to concentrate all day. She had an uneasy sense that something terrible had happened. She told herself she was being ridiculous, but she couldn't shake the feeling.

She felt a light pat on her hand and gazed into Kimi Foley's tear-filled blue eyes. The four-year-old was still struggling to master sign language, and today's lesson had been frustrating for both of them. Allie's attempts to get either of her parents involved had failed miserably. The Foleys had also been reluctant to let their oldest daughter step in and take the lessons so that she could help Kimi.

"What's wrong with me?" she signed, her expression miserable.

"Oh, baby," Allie whispered, then signed, "Nothing is wrong with you. You are very special."

Kimi's hands moved hesitantly, then fell still as

she searched for some way of expressing her feelings. Tears rolled down her cheeks. Even without the words, Allie understood.

"Sweetheart, you are going to have all the words you need one of these days. I promise."

"My friends," she began, then stopped, clearly struggling to go on.

"What about your friends?" Allie encouraged.

"They don't play with me," she signed with a weary little sigh, then crawled into Allie's lap for comfort. Her arms crept around Allie's neck.

Choked up by the child's obvious pain, Allie wondered if her parents had any idea what they were doing to her. If the isolation of sudden silence was overwhelming for a nineteen-year-old, as Allie had been, what must it be like for a little girl who'd lost her hearing when she was barely able to speak and whose vocabulary was limited?

She glanced up to find Kimi's father standing in the doorway, his expression anguished.

"What's wrong?" he asked. "Is she okay?"

"She says her friends won't play with her," Allie told him. "Most likely it's because they don't know how to talk to her, so they just stay away."

"My God," he whispered, then tapped Kimi on the shoulder and held out his arms. His daughter scrambled into them and buried her head on his shoulder. He looked at Allie. "What do I do?"

"It would help if you and your wife, maybe even your children, would take the sign language classes. At least Kimi would be able to communicate at home."

He nodded. "We'll do it. I hadn't realized how

she must feel. I wanted so badly to pretend that she was normal.''

"She *is* normal,'' Allie said fiercely. "She just can't hear.'' She regarded him intently. "Do you think I'm normal?''

He looked dismayed by the question. "Of course.''

"One day Kimi will be able to communicate just as well. Although she may not have the verbal skills, because she was so young when she lost her hearing, she will have compensated in other ways. But she needs your help now for that to happen.''

"She'll have it,'' he said with grim determination. "I'm not sure how we'll manage it, but we will.''

Allie walked with them to the front door, then smiled at him. "I will do whatever I can to accommodate a schedule that works for you.'' She tucked a finger under Kimi's chin. "See you soon,'' she signed.

Kimi mimicked the gestures. And, his big hand awkward, her father did the same. A slow smile spread across Kimi's face.

As the father and daughter left, Allie breathed a sigh of relief. For the first time in weeks, she felt confident that things were going to work out.

When she turned to go back to her office, she found Gina waiting for her.

"Come with me,'' her boss signed, her expression somber.

"My next patient's due in a few minutes.''

"Carol's taking her,'' Gina said.

Alarm flared at once. Allie's heart began an unsteady rhythm. Although the instructors occasionally backed each other up with patients, Gina usually pre-ferred the same therapist to work with each one.

Unless there was an emergency.

Allie's pulse was racing by the time Gina closed her office door.

"What is it? Is it one of my parents?"

Gina shook her head.

"Oh, my God," she said, sinking onto a chair. "It's Ricky, isn't it? The earthquake in China. Maria told me he had to go. What's happened?"

"There was a cave-in at the building he was searching. He was trapped in it."

Tears spilled down her cheeks. "Is he…?" She couldn't even bring herself to complete the question.

"Tom called Maria. He says Ricky is alive, but he's been pretty seriously hurt. The doctors over there are still checking him out. There could be in-ternal injuries, but the worst of it seems to be a blow he took to the head from a steel beam that shifted. He's been unconscious since they pulled him out. They'll know more in a few hours. Tom's been at the hospital the whole time. He's keeping in touch with Maria. If you want to be at home with the fam-ily, we'll cover for you here."

Obligations warred with the terrible need to know whatever news there was the instant it was available.

"I should stay," she began, but Gina cut her off.

"You should be with Ricky's family, at least until you get some further word. You can decide tomor-row if you're ready to come back in."

Dazed, she nodded. "Yes, that's probably best. I'd be useless this afternoon, anyway."

"Call me and let me know what's happening," Gina said. "I'll be praying for him."

Allie nodded, then raced to get her purse and head for Maria's.

The whole family had gathered there by the time she arrived. No one seemed the least bit surprised by her rush to be with them. First Maria and then Mrs. Wilder pulled her into a tight embrace.

"He's going to be fine," Mrs. Wilder said, her expression set stubbornly. "Our Enrique is strong."

"Of course he is," Allie agreed. "Hardheaded, too."

That drew a smile from the older woman. "Who should know that better than you and I, right, *niña*. He loves us, and that will make him fight to come back to us."

Allie glanced at the TV, saw that it was tuned to a station that was reporting the tragedy. There was a clip showing the efforts to get Ricky out of the building, then another one as they loaded his still body into an ambulance. Filled with dread, Allie turned away.

*Don't you dare die,* she raged inside. *You have to come back to me. You have to!*

Suddenly she understood the decision that Nikki had reached to take Tom back into her life. Allie realized it wouldn't matter whether she married Ricky or not. She would always be terrified when he was away, would always wait anxiously until he came back home. If that was true, then why let her fear cost them whatever precious time they might be allowed? She just prayed she would have a chance to tell him.

A few minutes later Nikki arrived, along with an official from the fire department. Mrs. Wilder and Maria headed for the kitchen and began cooking. Allie followed them, needing their presence as reassurance that everything would turn out okay. Those two women, more than anyone else in the house, believed it with all their hearts. Allie wanted to share their faith, but the arrival of the fire department official scared her. She was fearful that he had come because he was anticipating bad news.

"Sit," Maria ordered. "You're pale as a ghost."

Allie did as she was told and accepted a glass of brandy, even though she almost never touched alcohol. Still, she took a sip of the amber liquid and felt the heat spread inside her.

One sip was enough, though. She put the glass aside, aware that Maria was studying her worriedly.

"I'll be okay," she assured her.

"Of course, you will," Mrs. Wilder said, patting her shoulder. "It's just that this came as a shock."

Tears welled up and spilled down her cheeks. "What if…?"

"None of that," Mrs. Wilder commanded. "The phone is going to ring and Tom will tell us that Ricky is awake and complaining like always."

She left the kitchen with a plate of sandwiches before Allie could respond. Allie stared after her with admiration. "She has such faith," she said to Maria. "I envy her that. I'm scared to death."

"Don't let her fool you. So is Mama, but she believes in God's mercy and in His goodness. She's counting on that to bring her son home safely."

"I pray she's right," Allie said.

"What will you do when he gets here?" Maria asked, her expression troubled. "I see the love shining in your eyes, but everything that has happened today has confirmed your worst fears, hasn't it?"

Allie nodded, grappling with the emotions that had welled up inside her since the minute Gina had delivered the terrible news. "But it's also proved something else," she said slowly, wanting to tell Maria about the decision she'd made.

"Proved what?"

"That I don't want to lose a single second of whatever time I could have with him. Nikki realized that about Tom. And Jane always knew it about her husband. I didn't understand what they meant when they first told me, but after today, I think I do."

Just then, her timing impeccable as always, Jane walked into the kitchen, her colorful attire like a ray of sunshine in the gloomy atmosphere. She opened her arms and gathered Allie close. "I saw on the news and came right over."

"We're not going to lose him," Allie said with a surprising surge of conviction. "He has too much to live for."

"Does he?" Jane asked, studying Allie with a penetrating look.

Allie nodded.

"That's news that will definitely get him back here," she said, winking at Maria. "Don't you think so?"

"Absolutely," Maria said just as the phone rang. She grabbed it. Her expression brightened almost at once. "Well, if it isn't my baby brother."

A sense of relief washed over Allie, and then Maria was pulling her close. "My brother would like to hear the sound of your voice."

Allie swallowed hard. "Enrique Wilder, you scared us half to death," she scolded.

Maria grinned at the response on the other end of the line, then said, "I will not tell her that."

"Tell me what?" Allie demanded.

"He says he didn't come back from the dead just to have you yell at him."

Allie chuckled, then spoke into the phone. "If you think that's yelling, just wait till I see you in person." Her voice faltered then as it sank in just how close she had come to losing him. "I love you," she whispered. "Just come home soon."

Then she turned away, put her head on Jane's shoulder and let the tears fall.

*I love you. Just come home soon.*

Ricky clung to Allie's words over the next few days. Impatient to get home and see her, he had to battle the doctors for permission to make the trip.

"Being with my family will be the best medicine," he told them, but to no avail. They were determined not to let him go until they had completed a dozen different tests, repeated them, analyzed the results and concluded that he wouldn't die en route. He could have told them that there was no way he was going to die, not when Allie was waiting for him half a world away, but he doubted they would buy his assessment of his prognosis.

It was Tom who finally persuaded them to let him go, but only after mustering the resources to get Ricky onto a medical transport flight that would take him home with a nurse in attendance.

"Thank you," he told his best friend.

"Hey, nobody's more anxious than I am to get you back to the States. You are not a good patient.

I'm more than ready to turn the hovering over to Allie and your mom.''

"You're staying?"

Tom nodded. "The job's not done. Give Nikki a kiss for me and tell her I'll be home to help her plan that wedding soon."

Ricky grinned. "Maybe we can make it a double ceremony."

"Why Allie would want to marry a stubborn cuss like you is beyond me, but if she does say yes, we'll give it a shot," Tom agreed. "Maybe that way at least one of us will actually remember our anniversary and keep the other one out of trouble."

"Now that *is* an incentive," Ricky agreed. He regarded his longtime partner soberly. "I owe you, pal. I know you moved heaven and earth, just about literally, to get me out of there. I wouldn't be here if it weren't for you."

"The whole team was there every second. You're one of us. We weren't about to lose you. Now go home and get well so I don't have to shoulder your load the next time we get a call."

Soon after Tom left the plane, the nurse brought Ricky the pain pills he'd been refusing for days now. She persuaded him to take them by reminding him that it was going to be a long flight and he'd want to be well rested when he got back to Florida.

"You don't want to scare your family half to death when they see you, do you?"

Because the jostling he'd taken en route to the airport had sharply reminded him of every single ache and pain in his body, he gave in. A couple of pain pills would wear off long before they reached home. He intended to be wide-awake and fully alert when he saw Allie. He wanted to remember every single thing about their reunion. Not only that, if he proposed and she said yes, he didn't want her to be able to claim later that he'd asked while in a drug-induced state.

He was out of it for most of the endless flight, but the minute the pilot informed them that they were an hour out of Miami, Ricky called the nurse over.

"Can you help me shave?"

"You want to look pretty for your wife?" she asked with a grin.

"I'm hoping she'll agree to be my wife."

She laughed. "Then you really do need a little sprucing up. Let's see what we can do."

There was only so much improvement that could be made because of the bandages, but Ricky thought the bright-turquoise Florida Marlins cap gave him a jaunty look. Given how Allie felt about the team, maybe it would help his cause.

As soon as the plane was on the ground, he spotted his entire family on the tarmac waiting for him, along with an ambulance ready to take him to a Miami hospital to be checked out thoroughly before he could be permitted to go home to his own bed, where he desperately wanted to be.

His gaze frantically searched the gathering before finally coming to rest on Allie. She was so beautiful, she took his breath away. She was the reason he'd survived, the thought that had kept him fighting to stay alive. Her words on the phone had given him hope. Not just the admission that she loved him, but the promise in her voice that she wouldn't take that love away ever again.

Of course, once she got a look at him, all broken

and bandaged, she might have second thoughts. He turned to the nurse. "What do you think? Can I get the girl looking like this?"

"Sugar, you'll sweep her off her feet. Just try to get past the black-and-blue stage before the wedding. It'll look lousy with the tux."

Ricky wished he could walk off the plane, but it was out of the question. He was carried out on a stretcher, the transporters pausing at the base of the steps to let his family surround him. His sisters hugged him gingerly, tears spilling onto his face.

"Hey, cut the waterworks," he pleaded. "I'm not dead, and you're ruining the outfit."

"Move out of my way," his mother chided her daughters, shouldering them aside to bend down and press a kiss to his cheek. She murmured to him in Spanish, then crossed herself and added a quick prayer.

"I'm going to be okay, Mama."

She winked at him. "I never doubted it. You have a reason for living. *¿Sí?*"

Ricky's gaze met Allie's and he nodded slowly. "Yes, I definitely have a reason for living."

"We will leave you with Allie now and see you later at the hospital," she promised, then leaned down to whisper. "Don't waste a minute, *niño*. I think she is ready to say yes."

Ricky grinned. "I hope you're right, Mama."

Allie looked from him to his mother. "Right about what?"

His mother patted her cheek. "It is not polite to eavesdrop."

After the others had gone, Ricky gazed into Allie's eyes. "Come here," he commanded quietly.

She stepped closer, her eyes bright with unshed tears, and took his one unbandaged hand in hers. "You had to go and prove me right, didn't you?" she chided.

"*I* was right," he contradicted. "I told you I'd always come home, no matter what."

"Then I guess you win," she said.

Hope rose up inside him. "Oh?"

"That is if you still want me."

The pain, which had been dulled for a while by the pills, came back full force, but he fought it. The moment was too sweet to let anything ruin it. He drew in a deep, relaxing breath and focused on her. "You're saying yes?"

"I thought I was the one who couldn't hear," she teased.

He reached up and touched her cheek gently. "Can you hear what my heart is saying now?" he said, his gaze locked with hers.

She rested her hand against his chest, where she had to be able to feel the steady, reassuring beat of his heart.

"I believe I can," she said.

"It's beating because I knew I had to get back to you, because I promised. You're the reason I'm alive. Now we're even."

Her tears spilled over. "I was so scared," she whispered.

"I can't swear to you that it will never happen again," he told her honestly. "But I love you, Allie. I want us to have years and years together with kids of our own who are as smart and brave as their mother."

She gave him a watery smile. "Smart, maybe,"

she teased. "But brave? I don't know about that. You're the strong one."

He tucked a finger under her chin. "No. It's always harder being left behind than it is to be taking the risks. I know that."

"And I know that it wouldn't be any easier if I walked away now. I would always wonder and worry. You're in my heart, Enrique Wilder, for better or for worse."

"Tom wants to have a double wedding," he told her. "What do you think?"

"Anytime, anyplace," she said. "I don't want to waste another minute."

As if to prove it, her mouth settled lightly against his. Ricky was pretty sure that kiss could heal whatever injuries he had. It definitely would be a potent incentive for never taking an unnecessary risk.

"Ricky," she murmured when she pulled away, looking a little dazed. "I think you've given me back my music."

"Oh?"

A smile spread across her face. "I'm pretty sure I heard bells."

He laughed. "I know I did, *querida*. I know I did."

## *Epilogue*

Allie still couldn't get over the way her mother had gotten into the spirit of the wedding preparations. She had insisted on taking off the spring semester and coming to Miami a month ahead of time. She had taken up residence in the guest room at Ricky's. She'd made no comment at all about the fact that Allie was living in the master bedroom with her fiancé.

In fact, she seemed to approve of her prospective son-in-law from the instant they met. Allie constantly found them with their heads together, looking through the replacement photo albums she'd brought, filled with some of the same pictures that had been lost in the hurricane. Allie knew that Ricky and Jane had had a hand in the creation of those albums and she was touched. Her mother couldn't have brought a better wedding present.

But if the instant bond between her mother and Ricky was a surprise, more shocking was the immediate connection the very staid Grace Matthews had formed with the exuberant Mrs. Wilder. They had designated themselves in charge of the planning for the double ceremony, leaving little for Allie or Nikki to do. Once in a long while, her mother consulted Allie about her preferences for this hors d'oeuvre or that one, but in general she seemed to be having the time of her life.

Allie observed all this with mounting confusion. What had happened to the woman she knew, the woman who preferred faculty teas to family dinners, the woman who had difficulty expressing her feelings?

Finally she insisted on taking her mother to lunch to get an explanation. Her mother seemed startled and vaguely insulted by her questions.

"You're my only child. Why wouldn't I want to be involved in your wedding?"

Allie struggled to come up with an explanation for her confusion that wouldn't hurt her mother's feelings. "Ever since I moved down here, you and dad have been...I don't know how to put it. Distant, I suppose. After the hurricane you seemed almost relieved when I told you it wasn't necessary for you to come down to take care of me."

Despite her careful wording, her mother looked crushed. "Oh, darling, I am so sorry you felt that way. We were just so terrified of hovering the way we did when you first lost your hearing. We thought that would make things worse for you. And when you said you were doing fine, we felt we had to take you at your word."

Tears filled her eyes. "Don't you know that it was agony for us to have you in the hospital so far away after such a tragedy? When you told us you didn't need us? It would have been so easy to insist you come home where we could look out for you or to rush down here to coddle you. But if we'd done that, you might never have fought so hard for your independence." She managed a faint smile. "You might never have gotten involved with Ricky."

Allie was stunned by the explanation. "You did it for *my* sake? I mean not just lately, but staying away when I first moved here?"

"Well, of course. Why else?"

"I was afraid you were disappointed in me, maybe even ashamed. I thought you were glad I'd gone so far away."

The tears in her mother's eyes spilled down her cheeks. "Allison Matthews, your father and I could never be disappointed in you," she declared indignantly. "We were devastated when you lost your hearing. We blamed ourselves for not taking better care of you. Of course it saddens us that you lost your music, but for *your* sake, not ours. We've loved you from the instant you were born. And we have never been more proud of you than we are now."

She swallowed hard, clearly struggling for composure. "You're remarkable, Allie. Can't you see that? Years ago you took a great tragedy and turned it into a challenge, which you have more than met. You did that again after the hurricane. You've found a truly wonderful man who obviously loves you. I expect we'll have gorgeous grandchildren we can dote on in no time. I've never seen you look happier.

What more could a parent possibly want for a child?''

Her own eyes stinging with tears, and suddenly feeling as if her entire world was right again, Allie reached across the table and squeezed her mother's hand. ''I love you, Mom.''

In an afternoon of surprises, her mother responded in sign language. ''I love you, my darling daughter.''

That night as she snuggled close to the man who would be her husband in a few days, Allie recounted the story.

''I'm happy for you,'' he said. ''I know how much you wanted your family around, even though you stuck that brave little chin of yours up in the air and declared it didn't matter if they were.''

''My hunch is that if we give them a grandchild, we'll have a hard time getting rid of them.''

He pulled her astride him, then grinned as he began to move inside her for the second time that night. ''By all means, then, let's give them what they want.''

Ricky stood next to Tom at the front of the church his family had attended his entire life, tugging at the tight collar of his fancy shirt.

''Remind me never again to wear one of these things,'' he grumbled.

''You say that at every wedding,'' Tom pointed out.

''Well, thank goodness there are no more sisters or best friends to get married. I should be safe.''

''Only till all those nieces and nephews grow up,'' Tom retorted just as the music began.

Ricky turned to watch as his sisters started down

the aisle in their pastel bridesmaid gowns. Nikki and Allie had agreed that they both wanted the Wilder women as their attendants. In fact, they had agreed on every single detail. He had a hunch that all Nikki cared about was getting Tom's ring back on her finger. She hadn't even batted an eye when Allie had insisted on having Jane as her matron of honor. As for Jane, she had been moved to tears by the request.

Now as Jane reached the front of the church, she gave Ricky an impudent wink, then took her place as the music swelled and everyone turned to watch for the brides. He peeked at Jane's feet, but, for once, to his disappointment, she wasn't wearing her bright sneakers.

Then his attention was riveted to the back of the church as the organist shifted into the familiar notes of "Here Comes the Bride."

Nikki came down the aisle first, wearing a simple white satin cocktail-length dress and carrying a bouquet of orchids, her gaze locked with Tom's all the way.

Then Allie appeared in the arched entryway, resplendent in a simple gown of white silk with tiny pearls around the scooped neckline. The narrow skirt fell to the floor, then extended in back to a short train. Rather that wear a tiara and veil, she had opted to have a strand of pearls woven into her upswept hair. Ricky hid a smile as he spotted the errant curls that had already escaped the tamed style to caress her cheeks.

"I might not hear the words, so I want to see everything very clearly," she had told him. "A veil would just get in the way."

He watched as she glanced up at her father, who

gently patted her hand where it was looped through his arm. Then she focused all her attention on the cadence of Nikki's steps. Her lips pursed, and he knew she was humming the music as she began her walk down the aisle on her father's arm, a sweet-smelling bouquet of roses and camellias clutched in her hand. Misty-eyed, her father kissed her cheek before he released her into Ricky's care.

Ricky hadn't told her in advance what his intentions were, but he saw the joy begin to shine in her eyes when the minister accompanied the words of the ceremony with sign language. Ricky repeated his own vows, not only speaking them but signing them.

"So you will hear them well," he told her. "And keep them in your heart forever."

"Next to the love I have for you," she told him.

Then her voice rang out clearly in the old, Spanish-style church, promising to love, honor and cherish him, "all the days of our lives. Whether they be many or few, I will be grateful for each one."

And then, to his surprise and his family's evident delight, she repeated the vow in halting Spanish.

She made the commitment with such love shining in her eyes, such a solemn tone to her voice, that Ricky knew he would do everything in his power never to let her down.

"We'll be together through eternity," he mouthed softly, and saw her lips curve into a smile.

That smile said more than a thousand words.

At the reception after the ceremony, Tom and Nikki took them aside. Tom looked as if he were in shock.

"We have something to tell you," Nikki said, her

face radiant. "I just told Tom after the ceremony, so excuse him if he seems a little dazed."

"What?" Allie said, her gaze intent on her friend's face.

Nikki beamed. "I'm pregnant."

"Oh, my gosh," Allie said, a grin spreading across her face. "You must be ecstatic."

"I am," Nikki confirmed. Her expression sobered a little as she glanced at her new husband. "I'm not so sure about him."

"It's still sinking in," Tom said. "Me, a father? I can't believe it. I guess this means I'm about to change jobs."

At Ricky's startled look, he shrugged. "I promised her I'd do it when we started a family. We're just a few years off our timetable."

"You actually don't seem all that upset about it," Ricky noted.

Tom's expression turned thoughtful. "You know, I can't honestly say that I am. After what happened to you on that last trip, I began to see why Nikki was so shaken every time I left home. You scared the dickens out of me, too. I've been thinking the last few weeks that maybe I've had enough thrills and lived to tell about it. There's no point in pressing my luck, not when I have so much to live for."

Ricky gave Nikki a kiss, then hugged his friend. "Congratulations, you two. I'm really happy for you. I'm going to miss you at work, though. It takes a long time to find someone you're willing to trust with your life."

"There are plenty of guys on the team ready to step into my place. You'll be fine."

Ricky glanced at Allie and knew her doubts were

being magnified a hundredfold by Tom's announcement. When the other couple had walked away, he tucked a finger under her chin.

"Hey, don't look so worried. I made you a promise. I intend to keep it."

"You'd better," she said fiercely. "I expect to have years and years with you. Besides, it takes time to have all those kids we've been talking about."

He grinned. "Want to sneak out of here and get started?"

She gestured toward the cake, which still hadn't been cut, and the band, which was just getting ready to start playing. "I think we'd be missed. Besides, you promised to teach me to tango tonight."

"The tango is a very seductive dance," he pointed out. "I could give you an even more amazing lesson in the privacy of the bridal suite upstairs."

"No band."

He slipped his arms around her waist and pulled her close. "We won't need one."

"Hey, it's bad enough that one of us can't hear the music," she teased.

"Not true," he said, his gaze locked with hers. "The music's in here, *querida*." He tapped his chest. "And I can hear it loud and clear."

Her lips curved slightly, and she tilted her head as if listening intently. "Come to think of it, so can I."

\* \* \* \* \*

*And starting in May 2001, from
Silhouette Special Edition, watch for
an exciting new miniseries
by Sherryl Woods*

## THE CALAMITY JANES

*These five friends were social disasters
in high school. Now they're coming home
again, and it looks as if their
luck's about to change.*

*Now turn the page for a
sneak preview of the first title
in this compelling new series,*
*DO YOU TAKE THIS REBEL?*

## Chapter One

The thick white envelope had all the formality of a wedding invitation. Cassie weighed it in her hands, her gaze locked on the postmark—Winding River, Wyoming. Her hometown. A place she sometimes longed for in the dark of night when she could hear her heart, instead of her common sense, when hope outdistanced regrets.

Face facts, she told herself sternly. She didn't belong there anymore. The greatest gift she'd ever given to her mother was her leaving. Her high school friends—the Calamity Janes, they'd called themselves for their penchant for broken hearts and trouble—were all scattered now. The man she'd once loved with everything in her, well, who knew where he was. More than likely, he was back in Winding River, running the ranch that would be his legacy from his powerful, domineering father. She hadn't asked, because to do so would be an admission that he still mattered, even after he'd betrayed her, leaving her alone and pregnant.

Still, she couldn't seem to help the stirring of anticipation that she felt as she ran her fingers over the fancy calligraphy and wondered what was inside. Was one of her best friends getting married? Was it a baby announcement? Whatever it was, it was bound to evoke a lot of old memories.

Finally, reluctantly, she broke the seal and pulled out the thick sheaf of papers inside. Right on top, written in more of that intricate calligraphy, was the explanation: a ten-year high school reunion, scheduled for two months away at the beginning of July. The additional pages described all of the activities planned—a dance, a picnic, a tour of the new addition to the school. There would be lots of time for reminiscing. It would all be capped off by the town's annual parade and fireworks on the Fourth of July.

Her first thought was of the Calamity Janes. Would they all be there? Would Gina come back from New York, where she was running her fancy Italian restaurant? Would Emma leave Denver and the fast-track she was on at her prestigious law firm? And even though she was less than a hundred miles away, would Karen be able to get away from her ranch and its never-ending, back-breaking chores? Then, of course, there was Lauren, the studious one who'd stunned them all by becoming one of Hollywood's top box office stars. Would she come back to a small town in Wyoming for something as ordinary as a class reunion?

Just the possibility of seeing them all was enough to bring a lump to Cassie's throat and a tear to her eye. Oh, how she had missed them all. They were as different as night and day. Their lives had taken wildly divergent paths, but somehow they had always managed to stay in touch, to stay as close as sisters despite the infrequent contact. She would give anything to see them, but it was out of the question. The timing, the cost…it just wouldn't work.

"What are those, Mom?" Cassie cast a startled look at her son. Jake's attention was caught by the papers she was holding.

"Just some stuff from Winding River," Cassie said. "They're having a reunion this summer and I'm invited."

His expression brightened. "Are we gonna go? That would be so awesome. We hardly ever go to see Grandma. I was just a baby the last time."

She'd never had the heart to tell him that it was because his beloved grandmother liked it that way. As dearly as Edna Collins loved Jake, his illegitimacy grated on her moral values. At least she placed the blame for that where it belonged—with Cassie. She had never held it against Jake.

"I'm sorry, kiddo. I don't think so."

"But, Mom—"

"I said no, Jake, and that's the end of it." To emphasize the point, she tore up the invitation and tossed it in the trash.

Later that night, regretting the impulsive gesture, she went back to get the pieces, but they were gone. Jake had retrieved them, no doubt, though she couldn't imagine why. Of course, Winding River didn't mean the same thing to him that it did to her— mistakes, regrets and, if she was being totally honest, a few very precious, though painful, memories.

Her son didn't understand any of that. He knew only that his grandmother was there, the only family he had other than his mom. If Cassie had had any idea just how badly he missed her or just how far he would go for the chance to see her again, she would have burned that invitation without ever opening it. By the time she found out, Jake was in more trouble than she'd ever imagined getting into and her life was about to take one of those calamitous turns she and her friends were famous for.

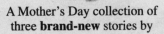

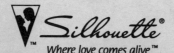

Silhouette Books and
award-winning, bestselling author

# LINDSAY MᶜKENNA

are proud to present

## MORGAN'S MERCENARIES:
### IN THE BEGINNING...

These first stories

## HEART OF THE WOLF
## THE ROGUE
## COMMANDO

introduce Morgan Trayhern's *Perseus Team*—
brave men and bold women who travel
the world righting wrongs, saving lives...
and resisting love to their utmost.
They get the mission done—but rarely escape
with their hearts intact!

*Don't miss these exciting stories available in April 2001—
wherever Silhouette titles are sold.*

# Silhouette®

## where love comes alive—online...

## eHARLEQUIN.com

### shop eHarlequin

- ♥ Find all the new Silhouette releases at everyday great discounts.

- ♥ Try before you buy! Read an excerpt from the latest Silhouette novels.

- ♥ Write an online review and share your thoughts with others.

### reading room

- ♥ Read our Internet exclusive daily and weekly online serials, or vote in our interactive novel.

- ♥ Talk to other readers about your favorite novels in our Reading Groups.

- ♥ Take our Choose-a-Book quiz to find the series that matches you!

### authors' alcove

- ♥ Find out interesting tidbits and details about your favorite authors' lives, interests and writing habits.

- ♥ Ever dreamed of being an author? Enter our Writing Round Robin. The Winning Chapter will be published online! Or review our writing guidelines for submitting your novel.

All this and more available at
**www.eHarlequin.com**
on Women.com Networks

SINTB1R

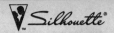

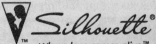